RETURN OF THE JEDI

EPISODE I: THE PHANTOM MENACE
EPISODE II: ATTACK OF THE CLONES
EPISODE III: REVENGE OF THE SITH
EPISODE IV: A NEW HOPE
EPISODE V: THE EMPIRE STRIKES BACK
EPISODE VI: RETURN OF THE JEDI

LAST OF THE JEDI

STAR WARS

EPISODE VI

RETURN OF THE JEDI

Ryder Windham
Based on the story by George Lucas and the screenplay
by Lawrence Kasdan and George Lucas

LUCAS BOOKS

SCHOLASTIC INC.
New York   Toronto   London   Auckland   Sydney
Mexico City   New Delhi   Hong Kong   Buenos Aires

www.starwars.com
www.scholastic.com

ISBN-13: 978-0-439-68126-1
ISBN-10: 0-439-68126-X

24 23 22 21 20 19 18 17 16 15 14 1   10 11 12 13 14 15 /0

Printed in the U.S.A.
First printing, October 2004

A long time ago, in a galaxy far, far away. . . .

After the destruction of the Death Star, the Sith Lord Darth Vader became obsessed with finding Rebel pilot Luke Skywalker. Vader almost caught him on the ice planet Hoth, but Luke — hoping to learn more about the Jedi arts — fled to Dagobah, where he trained with the aged Jedi Master Yoda.

With the aid of the bounty hunter Boba Fett, Darth Vader captured Luke Skywalker's friends and used them as bait to lure Luke into a trap on Cloud City. Despite Yoda's admonishments, Luke went to save them, only to be brutally wounded in a lightsaber duel with Vader. The Sith Lord further stunned his adversary with the declaration that he was really Luke's father. Vader's claim was all the more shocking because Luke's trusted mentor Ben Kenobi — the Jedi Master formerly known as Obi-Wan Kenobi —

had once told Luke that his father had been murdered by Vader.

Luke managed to escape Vader's clutches, but not before his friend Han Solo — a slightly reformed smuggler — had been frozen in a block of carbonite and turned over to Boba Fett. After several run-ins with competing bounty hunters, Boba Fett delivered Han's frozen form to the vile gangster Jabba the Hutt on the sand planet Tatooine.

While Luke and his allies prepared to rescue Han, the evil Emperor Palpatine sent Darth Vader to a remote sector of space, where the Empire's most powerful secret weapon was now under construction. . . .

CHAPTER 1

The second Death Star was far from finished.

Suspended in a synchronous orbit of the gas giant Endor's forest-covered moon, the space station was — at its present stage — an immense exposed superstructure, only partially covered by armored plating. Enormous skeletal girders curled away from the completed areas, wrapping protectively around the internal reactor core that ran between the station's poles. Even in its unfinished state, it was obvious that the station would be sphere-shaped.

And like its predecessor, the station had a super-laser focus lens positioned in its upper hemisphere and a trench that ringed the equator. However, it had none of the former Death Star's design flaws. The redesigned superlaser would require mere minutes — not hours — to be recharged, and could be focused more finely, allowing it to fire at moving targets, such as capital ships. With a projected diameter of 160 kilometers and a substantial increase in firepower, the new Death Star would be not only larger than the original but also much more lethal.

An Imperial Star Destroyer arrived near the building site, then a *Lambda*-class shuttle and two TIE fighters dropped out of the Star Destroyer's main hangar. As the shuttle and its escorts traveled toward the Death Star, its captain spoke into a comlink: "Command station, this is ST Three-twenty-one. Code Clearance Blue. We're starting our approach. Deactivate the security shield."

From the Death Star, a controller answered, "The security deflector shield will be deactivated when we have confirmation of your code transmission. Stand by . . . you are clear to proceed."

"We're starting our approach."

On the shuttle, Darth Vader peered through a window at the monstrous assemblage. He thought, *Even if it succeeds where the previous Death Star failed, it is an infant's trinket compared to the power of the Force.*

As Vader's shuttle neared the space station's equatorial trench, its hinged port and starboard wings raised in preparation for landing. The TIE fighters peeled off, and the shuttle proceeded to enter a wide hangar, where it touched down on a gleaming black deck.

In the Death Star control room, the shield operators sat rigidly behind their consoles. A control officer turned from a viewport, faced one of the shield operators, and said, "Inform the commander that Lord Vader's shuttle has arrived."

"Yes, sir," the shield operator quicky replied.

The Death Star's commanding officer was Moff Jerjerrod, a tall, confident technocrat who had risen through the ranks of Logistics and Supply. Jerjerrod hurried to the hangar and walked quickly past the Imperial officers and white-armored stormtroopers who stood at attention before the landed shuttle. Despite his confidence, Jerjerrod swallowed nervously as the shuttle's landing ramp lowered. There wasn't a single Imperial soldier who hadn't heard about Darth Vader's predilection for strangling those who'd failed to carry out his orders. Jerjerrod had no intention of having his name added to Vader's list of kills.

Darth Vader strode down the ramp. From his head-concealing helmet to his shin-armored boots, he was a nightmarish figure, clad entirely in black. An outer robe fell from his shoulders to the floor behind him, and he swept onto the hangar deck like a malevolent shadow.

"Lord Vader," Jerjerrod said, "this is an unexpected pleasure. We're honored by your presence."

"You may dispense with the pleasantries, Commander," Vader said, not breaking his stride as he moved past the gathered troops. "I'm here to put you back on schedule."

Walking fast to keep abreast with the dark lord, Jerjerrod said, "I assure you, Lord Vader, my men are working as fast as they can."

"Perhaps I can find new ways to motivate them."

Jerjerrod stopped walking and promised, "I tell you, this station will be operational as planned."

Vader stopped, too. Turning to face Jerjerrod, he said, "The Emperor does not share your optimistic appraisal of the situation."

"But he asks the impossible," Jerjerrod replied. "I need more men."

"Then perhaps you can tell him when he arrives."

Jerjerrod was aghast. "The Emperor's coming here?"

"That is correct, Commander," Vader stated. "And he is most displeased with your apparent lack of progress."

Jerjerrod had been standing straight, but tried to stand even straighter as he said, "We shall double our efforts."

"I hope so, Commander, for your sake. The Emperor is not as forgiving as I am."

Vader turned and walked out of the hangar, leaving Jerjerrod behind.

Back on Tatooine, C-3PO had troubles of his own.

"Of course I'm worried," the protocol droid

replied to a question his astromech companion R2-D2 had asked. "And you should be, too. Lando Calrissian and poor Chewbacca never returned from this awful place."

The awful place was their destination: Jabba the Hutt's palace, a large fortress near the southwestern border of the Western Dune Sea. But as the droids trudged once again across the desert world's desolate terrain, R2-D2 was more optimistic about the fate of their friends. For one thing, Lando could take care of himself pretty well. Also, the droid knew that Chewbacca hadn't even arrived yet at Jabba's palace, although he didn't bother mentioning this detail to C-3PO. Sometimes, the less C-3PO knew, the better. The astromech droid rotated his domed head to whistle a timid response to his gold-plated companion.

"Don't be so sure," C-3PO said. "If I told you half the things I've heard about this Jabba the Hutt, you'd probably short-circuit."

Indeed, Jabba Desilijic Tiure was legendary for his vicious temper, endless greed, gruesome appetite, and fondness for violent entertainment. He had been the reigning crime lord in the Outer Rim Territories for hundreds of years, and his illegal enterprises included smuggling, glitterstim spice dealing, slave trading, assassination, and piracy.

Jabba's palace had been built around the ancient monastery of B'omarr monks, a mysterious religious order that believed in isolating themselves from all physical sensation to enhance the power of their minds; to achieve this, enlightened monks had their brains transplanted into nutrient-filled jars. Rumor had it that B'omarr monks still existed in the palace's lower levels. C-3PO wasn't in any hurry to find out if the rumors were true.

The palace was a cluster of domed cylindrical towers. The largest structure was an enormous citadel with a massive rust-encrusted iron door at its base. Hesitantly approaching the door, C-3PO asked, "Artoo, are you sure this is the right place?"

R2-D2 answered with an affirmative beep.

C-3PO looked for some kind of signaling device — a chime, bell, or comlink panel — but saw none. Glancing at R2-D2, he said, "I'd better knock, I suppose." C-3PO tapped lightly on the door, then stepped back and observed, "There doesn't seem to be anyone here. Let's go back and tell Master Luke."

A small circular hatch slid open on the door and a long mechanical arm rapidly extended through the hatch. At the end of the arm, there was a large electronic eyeball with a built-in vocoder. The eyeball — set within a bronze optical shutter — belonged to a surveillance droid, which glared at C-3PO and snapped, "Tee chuta hhat yudd!"

"Goodness gracious me!" C-3PO said. Facing the

electronic eyeball, he gestured to R2-D2 and said, "Artoo Detoowha . . ."

The surveillance droid's arm pivoted to turn its gaze on the R2 unit. R2-D2 beeped, and the eyeball jutted forward unexpectedly for a closer look. R2-D2 beeped and jumped back.

". . . bo Seethreepiowha," C-3PO continued, indicating himself, "ey toota odd mishka Jabba du Hutt."

Hearing his master's name, the surveillance droid made an inhuman chuckling sound. Then the mechanical arm and eyeball zipped back into the door, and the hatch slammed shut.

"I don't think they're going to let us in, Artoo," C-3PO said, turning to walk away. "We'd better go."

R2-D2 could tell C-3PO was eager to get away from the palace, but the astromech didn't budge from the closed door. Suddenly, there was a horrific metallic grinding noise and the door began to rise. The door was still opening as R2-D2 scooted under it and into the citadel's dark, cavernous entry.

"Artoo, wait," C-3PO called. "Oh, dear!" Reluctantly, he followed the little droid into the citadel, and saw his friend was already far ahead of him. "Artoo, Artoo, I really don't think we should rush into all this."

Suddenly, a spiderlike robot with spindly legs lurched out from the shadows and scuttled past

C-3PO. The robot carried a jar that contained a brain: a disembodied B'omarr monk. Frightened by the sight, C-3PO cried, "Oh, Artoo! Artoo, wait for me!"

As R2-D2 moved forward, hidden sensors in the hallway walls scanned his body. The sensors pinpointed the many sophisticated tools that were housed in R2-D2's frame, but didn't detect any concealed explosives or blasters. The sensors did notice what appeared to be a non-standard cylindrical device in R2-D2's dome, but since the object was not a projectile weapon or a bomb, the sensors let it pass.

R2-D2 kept moving through the darkness until he struck something hard. Backing up, he adjusted his optical sensors to see that he'd bumped into a large Gamorrean, a green-skinned porcine alien with a large-nostriled cartilaginous snout and upturned tusks. Suited in heavy armor, the Gamorrean loomed over the droid and grunted.

C-3PO came up fast behind R2-D2 and said, "Just you deliver Master Luke's message and get us out of here." Stopping beside R2-D2, C-3PO saw the Gamorrean guard, then saw a second Gamorrean guard emerge from the shadows and said, "Oh, my!" The iron door slammed shut behind them. C-3PO added, "Oh, no."

"Die Wanna Wanga!" rasped an alien voice from nearby. C-3PO turned to see the speaker: a tall, pale-skinned male Twi'lek with blazing red eyes. The Twi'lek wore a black silk robe and his two long *lekku* — tail-like appendages that grew out from the back of his head — were draped around his sloped shoulders.

"Oh, my!" C-3PO repeated. He bowed to the Twi'lek, then replied, "Die Wanna Wauaga. We — we bring a message to your master, Jabba the Hutt."

R2-D2 let out a series of quick beeps, prompting C-3PO to add, "And a gift." Surprised by this last detail, C-3PO glanced at R2-D2 and said, "Gift, what gift?"

The Twi'lek shook his head. "Nee labba no badda." Then he smiled, revealing a mouth filled with sharp teeth, and stepped closer to R2-D2. The Twi'lek's hands had long fingernails, and he reached down to caress the little droid's dome, clearly indicating that he would like to possess the gift himself with the words, "Me chaade su goodie."

R2-D2 recoiled from the Twi'lek's touch. The droid rotated his dome back and forth, effectively shaking his head, and let out a protesting array of squeaks.

C-3PO faced the Twi'lek and translated, "He says that our instructions are to give it only to Jabba himself!"

One of the Gamorreans grunted and snarled menacingly at the Twi'lek, making it clear that Jabba would be angered if he didn't receive the droid's message. The Twi'lek's eyes went wide with fear and anger.

Facing the Twi'lek, C-3PO gestured to R2-D2 and said, "I'm terribly sorry. I'm afraid he's ever so stubborn about these sort of things."

The Twi'lek glared at the droids, then said, "Nudd chaa," and motioned them toward a dark doorway. One of the Gamorrean guards tagged along as the droids followed the Twi'lek to a tunneled stairway.

C-3PO said, "Artoo, I have a bad feeling about this."

The Twi'lek's name was Bib Fortuna, and he was Jabba's chief lieutenant. But Bib was hardly loyal to his master, and secretly anticipated the day the Hutt would croak his last. Grumbling to himself, Bib led the droids and Gamorrean guard down a flight of steps and into the Hutt's throne room.

The throne room was a dimly illuminated chamber that was literally crawling with grotesque creatures, most of whom were intoxicated. Numerous aliens cavorted on an elevated bandstand and various smoke-filled nooks. Jabba himself rested his bulky, gluttonous form upon a broad dais, and lazily sucked on a pipe linked to a naal thorn burner.

Beside the burner sat Salacious Crumb, a small Kowakian monkey-lizard with small beady eyes, long pointed ears, and a nasty laugh. Behind Jabba stood a short Jawa, who held a long-stalked palm and gently fanned the air around the Hutt. To Jabba's right, a lovely green-skinned female Twi'lek named Oola perched at the edge of the dais. Oola was one of Jabba's many slaves, and she wore a collar around her neck — Jabba held the leash.

Bib left the droids standing beside a wide metal grating on the floor in front of Jabba, then stepped up onto the dais and whispered to the Hutt. Jabba chortled and blinked his bulbous eyes. When he was done laughing, he let his gaze settle on the two.

C-3PO bowed and said, "Good morning." Turning to R2-D2, he said, "The message, Artoo, the message."

Impatient, Jabba exclaimed, "Bo shuda!"

R2-D2 rotated his dome and aimed his holographic message projector into the air behind him. All eyes turned to see a light-generated three-dimensional image of a black-uniformed human male materialize within the throne room. Because of the way R2-D2 had positioned himself, the hologram appeared to be facing Jabba. At approximately three meters tall, the hologram was larger than life.

"Greetings, Exalted One," the figure in the hologram said. "Allow me to introduce myself. I am Luke Skywalker, Jedi Knight, and friend to Captain Solo. I know that you are powerful, mighty Jabba, and that your anger with Solo must be equally powerful. I seek an audience with Your Greatness to bargain for Solo's life."

Hearing this, Jabba and his crowd laughed heartily.

"With your wisdom," Luke's hologram continued, "I'm sure that we can work out an arrangement which will be mutually beneficial and enable us to avoid any unpleasant confrontation. As a token of my goodwill, I present to you a gift: these two droids."

"What did he say?" C-3PO asked with alarm.

Luke's hologram continued, "Both are hardworking and will serve you well." With that, the hologram flickered off.

"This can't be!" C-3PO cried. "Artoo, you're playing the wrong message."

Bib whispered again to Jabba. In Huttese, Jabba replied loudly, "There will be no bargain."

Hearing this, C-3PO muttered, "We're doomed."

Jabba continued, "I will not give up my favorite decoration. I like Captain Solo where he is." The Hutt gestured with his meaty right hand to the other side of the throne room. The two droids followed the direction of Jabba's gesture to a display alcove. There, a dark gray rectangular slab was suspended vertically by a force field, and a man's figure — the same color as the slab — was set like a low-relief statue. The man's eyes were squeezed shut, and his mouth a silent cry.

"Artoo, look!" C-3PO said. "Captain Solo. And he's still frozen in carbonite."

C-3PO had been present in the Cloud City carbon-freezing chamber when Darth Vader had orchestrated the freezing of Han Solo. Vader had used Han as a test subject to determine whether a human could survive the freezing process, as Vader had intended to freeze Luke as well. Luke had evaded freezing and had been rescued by his allies, but they'd been unable to stop Boba Fett from fleeing Cloud City with Han's frozen form.

Obviously, Boba Fett had collected Jabba's bounty for Han Solo. And Han had been hanging on Jabba's wall ever since.

R2-D2 let out a worried beep.

Jabba instructed the Gamorrean guard to take C-3PO and R2-D2 to the cyborg operations supervisor. Leaving the throne room, the Gamorrean marched the two droids down a shadowy passageway that was lined with holding cells. Cries from imprisoned creatures echoed off the cold stone walls.

"What could possibly have come over Master Luke?" C-3PO wondered aloud. "Is it something I did? He never expressed any unhappiness with my work." C-3PO saw a repulsive hand reach out between the bars of a cell door and try to grab him. "Oh! Oh!" the protocol droid exclaimed. "How horrid!" Trying to avoid the hand, he moved to the other side of the passage. A long tentacle snaked out from between the bars of another cell door, and C-3PO felt the tentacle wrap around his neck.

"Ohh!" he wailed as he pulled himself free.

R2-D2 beeped pitifully as they moved to a thick metal door at the end of the passage. The door slid up into the ceiling, revealing a boiler room filled with steam and noisy machinery. The guard motioned R2-D2 and C-3PO into the boiler room, where a second guard awaited them.

Proceeding through the chamber, C-3PO noticed a white-metal 8D8 smelting droid who operated a rotating vise; the vise held a power droid, and the 8D8 rotated the power droid into an inverted position. When the power droid's two legs were positioned above its upside-down body, the 8D8 lowered red-hot branding irons onto its blocky feet. C-3PO cringed as the power droid let out an agonized electronic screech.

A few steps beyond the rotating vise, they arrived before Jabba's cyborg operations supervisor: a tall, skeletal robot named Eve-Ninedenine, who stood before an ancient, rickety computer console. C-3PO was distracted by the horrific sight of a nearby humanoid droid who was stretched out on what appeared to be a vertical torture rack, which was slowly pumping up and down, tugging at the unfortunate victim's manacled limbs.

Looking up at C-3PO and R2-D2, Eve-Ninedenine said, "Ah, good. New acquisitions." The robot's synthesized female voice sounded as if it had been stolen from an elderly prison matron, and as she spoke, her hinged vocoder flapped up and down beneath her sharp metal chin. Sizing up C-3PO, Eve-Ninedenine said, "You are a protocol droid, are you not?"

"I am See-Threepio, Human Cy —"

"Yes or no will do," Eve-Ninedenine interrupted.

"Oh," C-3PO said. "Well, yes."

Ninedenine said, "How many languages do you speak?"

"I am fluent in over six million forms of communication and can readily —"

"Splendid!" Eve-Ninedenine said, cutting off C-3PO again. "We have been without an interpreter since our master got angry with our last protocol droid and disintegrated him."

Hearing this, and remembering the incident, one Gamorrean guard clutched his broad belly and chuckled.

"Disintegrated?" C-3PO gasped, his voice filled with panic. Then he heard a snapping sound from the torture rack, and turned to see the upper rack had lifted higher than its mechanical victim's limbs could extend. Sparks exploded from the poor droid's arm and leg sockets.

Eve-Ninedenine rotated her head to one of the Gamorreans and said, "Guard! This protocol droid might be useful. Fit him with a restraining bolt and take him back up to His Excellency's main audience chamber."

The Gamorrean shoved C-3PO toward the door. The golden droid yelled, "Artoo, don't leave me! Ohhh!"

R2-D2 let out a plaintive cry as the door closed. Then he rotated his dome and beeped angrily at Eve-Ninedenine.

"You're a feisty little one," Eve-Ninedenine said, "but you'll soon learn some respect. I have need for you on the master's sail barge. And I think you'll fill in nicely."

The smelting droid lowered the branding irons again on the upside-down power droid's feet, and again the power droid screeched. R2-D2, who'd visited many inhospitable places in his long lifetime, decided that Jabba's palace was the absolute worst.

If any other crime lord had received a slightly threatening holographic message from someone who claimed to be a Jedi Knight, the crime lord might have prepared to negotiate, flee to another planet, or surrender entirely. But Jabba was not just any other crime lord, so he decided to throw a party.

It was a lewd and noisy affair, with semi-clad alien females gyrating to the rhythms of the Max Rebo band. On the bandstand, Max Rebo — a blue-skinned Ortolan who played a Red Ball Jett organ — performed a relatively slow tune; he was accompanied by a froglike Shawda Ubb named Rapot-wanalantonee — everyone called him Rappertunie — who played the growdi, a combination flute and water organ. While the music played, the nubile Twi'lek Oola danced evocatively beside the fleshy rumblings of Yarna d'al Gargan on the floor in front of Jabba's dais. From his dais, Jabba kept his grip on

Oola's leash as he drooled and watched her green body move.

Although Jabba may have appeared carefree, he had taken at least two precautions against the possible arrival of Luke Skywalker. First, he had instructed Bib Fortuna to make sure Skywalker didn't set foot inside the palace. Second, he'd made sure that his party included one particularly well-armed guest: Boba Fett.

Wearing the helmet he'd inherited from his father, Boba Fett was completely concealed within his weapon-laden suit, which included wrist-rocket gauntlets, kneepad rocket dart launchers, spring-loaded boot spikes, a turbo-projected grappling hook, and a bulky missile-firing jet backpack. His preferred weapon was a BlasTech EE-3 blaster rifle that he'd modified to fire with one hand; it was rarely out of his grip.

Fett had done various jobs for Jabba over the years, starting when he was a young boy, primarily as an enforcer. To most debtors, the very idea of receiving a visit from the merciless bounty hunter was good enough reason to make sure they paid Jabba on time. Boba Fett stood near the alcove that displayed the carbonite-frozen Han Solo and surveyed the throne room.

To the bounty hunter, everyone in the palace was

a suspicious character, so all he could really do was stand back and watch for Skywalker. But Fett watched the band's three female alien backup singers, too. One of them, a beautiful red-haired ungulate in a form-fitting body glove, looked down from the stage and winked at him.

Boba Fett's presence was also noticed by C-3PO. Having encountered him before, the golden droid kept his distance.

The music came to a close and Rappertunie bowed his small, chubby head to the audience. Jabba tugged at Oola's leash and said in Huttese, "Ah! Do that again!"

One of Max Rebo's singers, a short, furry alien named Joh Yowza, thought Jabba was demanding another tune. In a deep, raspy voice, Yowza called out, "One, two, three!"

This prompted Rappertunie to start playing another song, but it wasn't the one Yowza wanted. Yowza shouted, "No, daddy, no! One, two, three!"

The entire band kicked in, and the three backup singers slinked onto the stage. The drunken audience hooted and yowled when lead singer Sy Snootles — a spindly-legged temptress with blue-spotted yellow-green skin — strutted out from behind the other singers and seized the microphone. Snootles' most notable physical feature was her mouth, which was at the end of a thirty-centimeter-long protrusion extending from her brightly mottled head. Her full, luscious lips were painted bright red.

Although Max Rebo had been leading his ensemble through a variation on a popular jizz-wailer standard, Sy Snootles slyly batted her long eyelashes and began belting out improvised lyrics that would have been officially banned by the Empire. Members of the audience found this amusing, except for the prudish Bib Fortuna, who was mortified. As for C-3PO, the protocol droid was completely bewildered by Sy Snootles' blatant misuse of several verbs.

While the music played, Jabba — with a lascivious gleam in his eye — beckoned Oola to come sit with him. The Hutt bellowed, "Da eitha!"

Oola stopped dancing and backed away, shaking her head. "Na chuba negatori Na! Na! Natoota . . ."

Furious, Jabba pulled hard at the leash, pointed to his dais, and commanded, "Boscka!"

Oola pulled back on the taut leash and continued to protest.

Jabba slammed his fist down on a button. Before Oola could step aside, a trapdoor opened beneath her and she plummeted through the floor. The musicians and singers went silent and looked to the spot where Oola had vanished. The trapdoor snapped shut and Jabba's cretinous friends hurried to peer down through the metal grating to view a deep pit below the floor.

Oola tumbled out of the hole and onto the dirt floor of the deep, high-walled pit. She rose quickly and stood to face a large iron door that was set into one of the pit's walls. Oola trembled as the door began to rise, and a muffled growl came from the other side. She knew what was coming, and that she was about to die, but she had already decided that death was preferable to spending one more moment as Jabba's slave.

While Jabba's friends looked down through the grating to watch Oola meet her doom, C-3PO shook his head and turned away. He glanced wistfully at the carbonite form of Han Solo, and wondered if he'd ever leave Jabba's palace in one piece.

Suddenly, there was the sound of blasterfire from a nearby stairway. C-3PO and everyone else turned to face the steps that led up to the citadel's main entrance. One of Jabba's bolder goons ran up the steps to find the source of the blasterfire, but a moment later he came falling back and landed in an unconscious heap on the floor.

Fett had heard the blast and seen the goon fall, but that sort of violence wasn't unusual in the palace. He returned his attention to Rystáll, the alluring singer who'd captured his attention and now stood close beside him, admiring his helmet. Using his helmet's targeting rangefinder, he kept an eye on the nearby stairway.

Two figures descended the steps and entered the throne room. The first was a bounty hunter completely clad in leather, including a head-concealing helmet with a metal speech scrambler and head bracket; the bracket was equipped with a vision-plus scanner and built-in targeting laser. In one leather-gloved hand, the hunter carried a long lance tipped with a shock blade. The other hand held a leash that was secured to a collar around the neck of the second figure: a tall, furry Wookiee, who appeared weak and dazed.

Keeping a firm grip on the leash, the masked hunter bowed to Jabba. Then, in a digitally scrambled male voice that sounded like a scratchy, guttural monotone, the hunter said in Ubese, "I am Boushh. I have come for the bounty on this Wookiee."

Hearing this, C-3PO peeked out from behind Jabba's henchmen and quietly cried, "Oh, no! Chewbacca!"

Jabba didn't speak Ubese, but he did recognize the captive Wookiee. From his dais, Jabba grinned and said, "At last we have the mighty Chewbacca."

The Hutt summoned C-3PO. Stepping up beside him, the protocol droid said, "Oh, us, yes, uh, I am here, Your Worshipfulness. Uh . . . yes!"

Jabba made a statement in Huttese. C-3PO turned to Boushh and translated, "Oh, the illustrious Jabba bids you welcome and will gladly pay you the reward of twenty-five thousand."

Boushh answered in Ubese, "I want fifty thousand. No less."

Turning to Jabba, C-3PO translated, "Fifty thousand. No less."

Aghast, Jabba flew into a rage. One of his thick arms lashed out and pushed the protocol droid, who fell off the dais and clattered to the floor below. Boushh casually transferred the lance from one hand to the other, so both the lance and leash were held in the hunter's right glove.

Rising from the floor, C-3PO muttered, "Oh, oh . . . but what, what did I say?"

Jabba addressed Boushh. As Jabba spoke, Boba Fett stepped away from Rystáll and moved to stand where he had a clear view of both Boushh and the Wookiee.

Jabba finished talking and looked at C-3PO. Switching back to Ubese, C-3PO faced Boushh and said, "Uh, the mighty Jabba asks why he must pay fifty thousand."

Boushh's left hand reached into an ammo pocket, removed a metal orb, and thumbed a switch on the orb. As a small light flashed at the switch's base, Boushh answered.

Cringing, C-3PO nervously translated, "Because he's holding a thermal detonator!"

Max Rebo covered his eyes with his stubby blue fingers, and Salacious Crumb — along with almost everyone else — dived for protective cover.

But Fett didn't hesitate, drawing his blaster rifle with incredible speed and aiming its barrel at Boushh. He recognized the thermal detonator as a Class-A type that would yield a blast radius of about twenty meters. He could also determine from the detonator's activation indicator light that Boushh had the trigger's control pins programmed to act as a deadman's switch: if Boushh's thumb came off the detonator's trigger, everyone and everything within the throne room — except for maybe a few pieces of Fett's armor — would be instantly disintegrated. Despite his reflexes, Boba Fett knew he wouldn't make it out of the room fast enough, but he wasn't about to die cowering on the floor.

A tense silence filled the throne room. Then Jabba the Hutt tilted his massive head back and began to laugh. When he caught his breath, he gestured to Boushh and said in Huttese, "This bounty hunter is my kind of scum . . . fearless and inventive."

Seeing that Jabba seemed to be in control of the situation, Fett lowered his blaster rifle slightly. Jabba made an offer to Boushh, which C-3PO translated: "Jabba offers the sum of thirty-five." Facing Boushh, the golden droid added, "And I *do* suggest you take it."

Boushh deactivated the thermal detonator and said, "Zeebuss."

"He agrees!" C-3PO exclaimed with immense relief. The throne room was filled with cheers and applause, and the raucous party resumed.

A pair of Gamorrean guards grabbed Chewbacca and hauled him out of the room. Boushh spoke briefly to C-3PO, then Bib Fortuna leaned in and muttered something about financial arrangements to Boushh. Bib stepped away, then both Boushh and C-3PO turned to see Boba Fett watching them from across the room. Fett slowly nodded his helmeted head to mutely acknowledge the other hunter.

Time and again, Fett had proven that he didn't have any real competition in the bounty hunter trade. However, Boushh had just demonstrated that even he could be caught unprepared.

Boba Fett was determined it wouldn't happen again.

The Gamorrean guards led Chewbacca down a curved stairway to the dungeon. But before the Wookiee left the throne room, he caught sight of an armored man who wielded a large vibro-ax. A bizarre helmet with a fang-adorned strap concealed the man's features, but Chewbacca saw through Lando Calrissian's disguise.

Lando had used an old underworld contact on Tatooine to secure a guard job at Jabba's palace, where he'd been assigned work — under the name Tamtel Skreej — on one of the Hutt's sand skiffs. It had pained Lando to watch the Gamorreans shove Chewbacca toward the doorway that led to the dungeon, but he let it happen because he knew the time had not yet come to fight.

Night fell on Tatooine, and darkness flooded Jabba's palace. When the drinks had all been poured and the last reveler had either left or passed out, a single figure stepped silently through the throne room. It was Boushh.

Boushh moved stealthily past a group of snoring, drunken creatures. Arriving before the display alcove, the bounty hunter looked up at the carbonite slab that contained Han Solo's frozen form. Below the slab, the floor was covered with sand. If there were any concealed security devices, Boushh did not see them.

Boushh stepped into the alcove and found two illuminated buttons on the wall, just below a curtained lift shaft. A press of the lower button deactivated the force field that held the slab suspended in the air. The slab slowly lowered to the floor — at least until it unexpectedly teetered and fell back, smacking against the wall with a loud thud.

Boushh glanced around and made sure that the nearby creatures were still sleeping. They were, and Boushh's attention returned to the slab that now leaned upright against the wall.

Control panels were set along the outer side edges of the carbonite frame. Boushh pressed a button beside the carbonite flux monitor, then slid the decarbonization lever and watched a green light flicker on the life system monitor.

The case began to emit a sound as the hard shell that covered the contours of Han's face began to melt away. Boushh watched bright energy spill out of the broken carbon shell. Sooner than expected, the metallic coat of carbonite drained off, and Han's slack body fell forward, away from the slab, collapsing on the sandy floor.

Boushh knelt beside Han and struggled to raise him. His hair and skin were wet and cold, and he was shaking all over.

Speaking in Basic, Boushh's scratchy, digitized voice said, "Just relax for a moment. You're free of the carbonite."

Han opened his eyes and reached for Boushh's mask.

"Shhh," Boushh said. "You have hibernation sickness."

"I can't see," Han said.

"Your eyesight will return in time," Boushh replied, helping him up to a sitting position.

Han continued to shake. "Where am I?"

"Jabba's palace."

"Who are you?"

Boushh reached up to remove the leather and metal helmet, revealing the face of Princess Leia. In her own voice, she said, "Someone who loves you."

"Leia!"

Leia kissed Han. She'd feared she'd never see him again, at least not alive, but here he was in her arms. For all the lost time, and because time was precious, she had to kiss him.

Then she remembered where they were. Her lips left his and she said, "I gotta get you out of here." She wrapped her arms around his torso and pulled him up to his feet.

Then they both heard a sound: a low, rumbling guffaw.

"What's that?" Han asked, straining his temporarily blinded eyes to seek out the source of laughter in the darkness. "I know that laugh."

Above the alcove, a curtain slid back from the lift shaft, revealing Jabba the Hutt and his chortling minions. Han and Leia slowly turned to face the crime lord. Salacious Crumb sat within the folds of Jabba's curved, meaty tail. Behind Jabba, C-3PO stood between Bib Fortuna and a three-eyed Gran named Ree-Yees. C-3PO had been unable to caution Leia because Ree-Yees' right hand was plastered over his vocoder.

Leia held Han close to her. Behind them, another curtain slid away from a stairway that led up to the palace's guest quarters. From the stairs, Boba Fett and Jabba's guards moved forward to the display alcove.

Han blinked his eyes and said, "Hey, Jabba. Look, Jabba. I was just on my way to pay you back, but I got a little sidetracked. It's not my fault."

"It's too late for that, Solo," Jabba said in Huttese. "You may have been a good smuggler, but now you're bantha fodder." Jabba laughed again, and Salacious Crumb joined in, cackling wildly.

Han said, "Look —"

"Take him away," Jabba ordered.

"Jabba . . ." Han said as he was seized by two guards and pulled away from Leia. "I'll pay you triple! You're throwing away a fortune here. Don't be a fool!"

As Han was hauled out of the room, a Gamorrean guard and the disguised Lando Calrissian came up on either side of Leia and gripped her arms. Jabba said, "Bring her to me."

The guards obeyed and escorted the princess so she was nearly up against the Hutt. Glaring at

Jabba, Leia said boldly, "We have powerful friends. You're going to regret this."

"I'm sure," Jabba slobbered. His tongue lolled out of his wide mouth and brushed against the side of her face and clothes.

"Ugh!" Leia said, recoiling.

C-3PO trembled and looked away. "Ohhh, I can't bear to watch," he cried.

Jabba thought Leia had a pleasant flavor, but he didn't care much for her drab, dusty clothes. He ordered Bib Fortuna to fetch some garments that were more to his taste. . . .

Jabba's guards brought Han down to the dungeon, shoved him into a cell, and locked the door behind him. In the middle of the cell's floor, there was a dirty puddle; Han splashed through it and nearly stumbled, but his groping hands caught the stone wall and he steadied himself. He still felt painfully cold and he couldn't stop trembling.

Suddenly, a growl came from the far side of the cell. Startled, Han jerked away from the sound, then he blinked his sightless eyes and said, "Chewie? Chewie, is that you?"

Chewbacca barked and stepped out from his shadowy corner. The Wookiee flung his furry arms around his friend.

Han said, "Chew — Chewie!"

Chewbacca barked some more.

"Wait, I can't see you, pal," Han explained. "What's goin' on?"

Chewbacca barked his reply.

There wasn't anything wrong with Han's hearing, and he couldn't believe what the Wookiee had just told him. "Luke?" Han said. "Luke's crazy. He can't even take care of himself, much less *rescue* anybody."

Chewbacca barked more.

"A — a Jedi Knight?" Han said with disbelief. "I'm out of it for a little while, everybody gets delusions of grandeur."

The Wookiee growled insistently. Then he hugged Han close to his chest and patted his head, trying to warm him.

"I'm all right, pal," Han said. "I'm all right."

But Chewbacca hadn't finished bringing Han up-to-date. He quickly informed Han that Lando Calrissian — who'd betrayed them to Darth Vader on Cloud City — had become their ally, and that Lando had already secretly infiltrated Jabba's palace.

If the information had come from anyone other than Chewbacca, Han would've never believed it. He found it difficult to imagine he could ever trust Lando again. But if they all got out of this mess alive, he was willing to give it a try.

The next morning, two Gamorrean guards were stationed in the dark entrance of Jabba's palace when the massive iron door began to rumble open. As the door lifted, bright sunlight poured in, revealing a solitary, silhouetted figure standing outside. The figure stepped through the doorway and into the cavernous hallway.

The hallway's hidden sensors scanned the figure: a human male who wore a black hooded robe. Beneath, the man was clad in a black tunic, pants, a leather belt, and boots. The sensors quickly determined he was not carrying any weapons . . . but he *did* have one unusual feature: his right hand appeared externally normal but was actually a fully functional mechanical replica. If this detail concerned Jabba's security system, it didn't stop the iron door from sliding shut behind the man.

When the man was halfway through the entrance hall, the two Gamorreans stepped out of the shadows and raised their axes to block his path. They'd expected him to surrender or run away, and were surprised when he stopped, raised a hand, and gestured at them. Both guards were instantly compelled to lower their weapons and fell back to their stations.

Luke Skywalker proceeded into the palace.

Once again, there was silence in Jabba's throne room. There had been another party, and more drinks and brain cells had gone the way of those previous. Behind Jabba's dais, C-3PO maintained a nervous watch over the sleeping bodies sprawled throughout the multileveled lair.

Leia, eyes closed, lay slumped beside Jabba's slumbering form. She had replaced Oola as Jabba's slave dancer, and was worried about the acrobatic dances she might have to perform. She wore a collar around her neck that was secured to a long chain. She also wore a skimpy costume that left very little of her unexposed to view. Salacious Crumb — who remained awake — leaned over from his resting spot within the curve of Jabba's tail and peeked at Leia's bare stomach.

Bib Fortuna was also awake. Hearing the sound of footsteps descending the stairway from the main entrance, he ran up and saw Luke coming down. The Twi'lek muttered in Huttese, telling Luke to leave immediately.

Luke simply said, "I must speak with Jabba."

Hearing these words, Leia opened her eyes and sat up. *Luke!*

On the stairway, Bib tried to hold off Luke. Shaking his tailed head, he said, "Shh. Ee toe seet. Jabba no two zand dehank obee. No pahgan."

Luke stared hard at Bib and said, "You will take me to Jabba now!"

Bib did not realize that Luke was using the Force to influence his thoughts. Reacting as if it had been his own idea to bring Luke to Jabba, Bib said, "Et tu takku u Jabba now," and motioned for Luke to continue down the stairs.

As Luke descended after Bib into the throne room, he said, "You serve your master well."

"Eye sota va locha," Bib agreed.

Luke added, "And you will be rewarded."

Leia saw Luke approach the dais but remained silent. From behind Jabba, C-3PO cried out, "At last! Master Luke's come to rescue me!"

Jabba's guards also noticed Luke's arrival and edged toward him cautiously. Bib Fortuna stepped up onto the dais, leaned close to the side of Jabba's broad head, and whispered, "Master."

Jabba's heavy eyelids slid back and he let out a wet snort. The noise awakened others in the room, who looked over to the dais to see what was going on. Jabba shifted his weight slightly, and Leia felt the slave collar tug against her throat.

Gesturing to Luke on the floor below the dais, Bib continued, "Luke Skywalker, Jedi Knight."

Outraged, Jabba said in Huttese, "I told you not to admit him."

"I must be allowed to speak," Luke insisted.

In Huttese, Bib said, "He must be allowed to speak."

"You weak-minded fool!" Jabba scowled. "He's using an old Jedi mind trick." Bib yelped as Jabba shoved him off the dais.

Luke sighted the disguised Lando among Jabba's guards. Several Gamorreans had moved up behind

Luke, but he remained outwardly calm and composed. He pulled back his hood to reveal his face. On the dais, Boba Fett emerged to stand beside the Hutt.

Staring hard at Jabba, Luke said, "You will bring Captain Solo and the Wookiee to me."

Jabba laughed. "Your mind powers will not work on me, boy."

He's stronger than I imagined, Luke realized. Moving closer to Jabba, he said, "Nevertheless, I'm taking Captain Solo and his friends. You can either profit by this . . . or be destroyed. It's your choice. But I warn you not to underestimate my powers."

C-3PO saw that Luke had stepped directly onto the trapdoor. "Master Luke," the droid called out, "you're standing on —"

But Jabba interrupted, "There will be no bargain, young Jedi. I shall enjoy watching you die."

Jabba's guards advanced toward Luke. Luke extended his right hand, and a guard's blaster suddenly jumped out of its holster and flew into Luke's waiting hand. As Luke raised the blaster to Jabba, a Gamorrean lunged at him, grabbing his arm.

Jabba shouted, "Boscka!" and brought his hand down on the trapdoor's control button. As the trapdoor opened, the Gamorrean squeezed Luke's arm and the blaster fired into the ceiling. Both Luke and the Gamorrean plunged into the pit beneath the throne room.

Jabba's dais slid forward across the floor, sealing the trapdoor.

Tumbling through the hole, Luke lost the blaster. He landed amidst the skeletal remains of various creatures. Expecting to fight the Gamorrean who'd fallen into the pit with him, he whipped off his black robe and rose to his feet. The Gamorrean was still rising when Luke glanced up at the bottom of the grating, where Jabba and his courtiers gazed down at him and laughed.

Luke saw Leia and C-3PO through the grating far above him. There was fear in Leia's eyes. Luke thought, *Don't be afraid, Leia! We're going to get out of here.*

Then there was a rumbling sound, and Luke looked to the pit's far wall, where a large iron door began to rise up into a slot in the rocky ceiling. A horrific growl echoed from a holding cave beyond the door, and the Gamorrean started squealing hysterically. From above, C-3PO cried out, "Oh, no! The rancor!"

Luke thought, *What am I up against now?* The door was still rising when he had his first glimpse of the monster's massive claws. Luke sensed that the rancor's ferocity matched its size, and his eyes went wide with alarm as the rancor hunched its form and pushed its way through the doorway.

Lurching into the pit on two powerful legs, the rancor revealed itself to be a reptile-like beast, roughly five meters tall. It had an enormous, fanged maw set beneath a pair of small glowing eyes. Its head and jaws seemed to take up most of its body; its two long arms ended in absurdly long, sharp talons. A broken chain dangled from a manacle at its right wrist.

The rancor opened its wide mouth and roared at the Gamorrean, who tried futilely to scramble out of the pit. Luke noticed the pit's walls bore deep scratches and claw marks from others who'd tried to escape the rancor and failed.

While Jabba and his cohorts cackled and jeered, the rancor reached out and snatched up the Gamorrean. The smaller creature kicked and squealed as the rancor popped him into its mouth. *Crunch!* The rancor tilted its head back and swallowed the guard, armor and all.

Then the monster turned for Luke. Above them, Jabba the Hutt smiled grotesquely.

The rancor swiped at Luke, but the young man jumped aside. A long arm-bone from an earlier victim lay on the pit floor, and Luke seized it. Suddenly, the rancor's talons wrapped around Luke's body and lifted him off his feet.

Luke clung to the bone as the rancor drew him to

its salivating mouth. The rancor's fangs were still slick with the Gamorrean's blood, and the stench of gore was almost overwhelming. With a sharp twist, Luke wedged the bone into the rancor's mouth, forcing its jaws back. Startled, the beast reflexively released Luke, who fell to the floor.

There was a loud snap, and Luke glanced up to see the rancor had crushed the bone. Luke found a small crevice in the pit wall and scurried into it. Gazing past the monster to the holding cave beyond, he spotted a utility door. *If I can just get to it . . .*

The hungry rancor saw Luke and reached into the crevice. Luke grabbed a large rock and smashed it down on the rancor's talon. The rancor howled.

Luke rolled out of the crevice and ran for the holding cave, which was littered with even more bones. He reached the utility door and pushed a button. The door slid open, but a heavy barred gate separated him from the adjoining chamber, in which two guards — the rancor's keepers — were playfully fighting over their dinner. They stopped fighting when they saw Luke. Luke turned to see the monster was still in the pit. He pulled with all his might on the gate but with no effect. On the other side of the gate, the two guards picked up spears and laughed as they poked at Luke, forcing him away.

As the rancor hunched down and prepared to enter the holding cave, Luke noticed a control panel halfway up the wall beside the doorway. Thinking fast, he picked up a skull from the cave floor and hurled it. The rancor was just ducking its head through the doorway when the thrown skull smashed against the control panel, destroying the iron door's lifting mechanism. The heavy door came crashing down upon the rancor's head, its sharp stakes pinning the monster to the floor.

There was a collective gasp from the watchers above. The rancor wasn't merely pinned; the door's pointed base had actually pierced and crushed the monster's skull. Its left talon flexed once, then went slack. The rancor was dead.

Breathing hard, Luke fell back against the wall of the holding cave. The rancor's keepers opened the gate and entered, passing Luke to examine their dead beast. One of the keepers broke down and wept. The other glared menacingly at Luke, who was unfazed.

Several guards immediately rushed into the holding cave and took Luke away. The guards were surprised and disappointed when Luke didn't resist.

Up in the throne room, Jabba was fuming. He couldn't believe that Luke had killed his prized rancor. Glowering at his guards, he commanded in Huttese, "Bring me Solo and the Wookiee. They will all suffer for this outrage."

The guards hurried out, and soon returned with

the two prisoners. From a different stairway, other guards — including Lando — dragged Luke into the throne room. As they were hauled before Jabba's dais, Luke shouted, "Han!"

"Luke!" Han called back. He still couldn't see, but he was pretty sure he could smell Jabba nearby.

"Are you all right?" Luke asked.

"Fine," Han replied. "Together again, huh?"

"Wouldn't miss it."

"How are we doing?"

Luke grinned. "The same as always."

"That bad, huh? Where's Leia?"

"I'm here," Leia said from Jabba's side. With the slave collar still tight around her neck, and Jabba stroking her like a domestic pet, she was almost relieved that Han was still blinded.

Boba Fett remained near Jabba and kept an alert watch on the captives while the Hutt began speaking in Huttese. C-3PO listened and said, "Oh, dear." As Jabba continued, C-3PO translated, "His High Exaltedness, the great Jabba the Hutt, has decreed that you are to be terminated immediately."

"Good," Han said. "I hate long waits."

Jabba prattled on, and C-3PO conveyed, "You will therefore be taken to the Dune Sea and cast into the Pit of Carkoon, the nesting place of the all-powerful Sarlacc."

Han leaned closer to Luke and muttered, "Doesn't sound so bad."

"In his belly," the protocol droid continued, "you will find a new definition of pain and suffering as you are slowly digested over a thousand years."

"On second thought," Han interjected, "let's pass on that, huh?"

As the guards hauled Chewbacca, Han, and Luke out of the throne room, Luke glared at the Hutt and said, "You should have bargained, Jabba. That's the last mistake you'll make."

Jabba laughed heartily and tugged the chain that held Leia, forcing her back against his slimy bulk. Leia thought, *This isn't going to end well, Jabba. Not for you!*

CHAPTER 4

Under a clear blue sky, a herd of wild, thick-furred banthas trekked across the western Dune Sea, the large area of sandy desert that stretched across the Tatooine wastes. Bound for a distant mesa, the banthas ignored the three repulsorlift vessels that passed in the distance. The vessels — one large and two small — glided several meters above the sand, heading north. Even the banthas knew better than to travel that way across the Dune Sea, if only to avoid the Great Pit of Carkoon.

The three craft were owned by Jabba the Hutt. The two smaller repulsorlifts were matching nine-meter-long open-topped cargo skiffs, which Jabba had had armor plated. Hardly more than flying platforms, the skiffs were without seats, so the pilot and passengers all stood on an exposed deck that was edged with a low protective railing. The first skiff flew as escort to the larger vessel and carried a group of Jabba's goons; the second skiff carried six guards — including Lando, in disguise — and three bound captives: Luke, Han, and Chewbacca.

The larger repulsorlift was Jabba's sail barge. Thirty meters in length, the *Khetanna* had been designed as a luxury pleasure craft, although most of its expensive trappings had been stripped years ago. Its two bright orange sails — primarily used as awnings to protect those on deck from the glare of Tatooine's suns — had faded considerably, and its hull and interior were mostly bare metal. What it lacked in comforts, however, it made up for with armor plating, a custom-mounted deck blaster cannon, plenty of room for Jabba's guests, and an extremely well-stocked kitchen. By any standards, the barge had style.

But Leia's standards were higher than most. *The sooner I get off this stinking death trap, the better.* She was inside the banquet room, located on the deck below the privacy lounge at the barge's stern. Because Jabba preferred the dry heat of Tatooine, the barge's air-conditioning system had been removed long ago and replaced with retractable window shutters. Still scantily clad, Leia sat beside an open window on the barge's port side and gazed at her captured friends on the skiff traveling alongside.

Jabba and his cronies were laughing and drinking heavily. Bounty hunter Boba Fett paced, instinctively eyeing the horizon for any signs of trouble. R2-D2 had been outfitted as an ambulatory bar, and was serving drinks — mostly spice-spiked flameouts and pink-and-green bantha blasters — from an elaborately decorated gold tray that wrapped around the back of his domed head. The Hutt downed another drink, then tugged at the chain attached to Leia's collar, just to remind her who was boss. Leia winced at the sharp jerk from the chain but clung to the edge of the window to keep her eyes on the skiff.

On the skiff, the captive trio stood close to one another behind a guard who was acting as lead lookout on the prow. Han squinted at the desert sky and said, "I think my eyes are getting better. Instead of a big dark blue, I see a big light blur."

"There's nothing to see," Luke said. "I used to live here, you know."

"You're gonna *die* here, you know," Han said. "Convenient."

"Just stick close to Chewie and Lando," Luke said, scanning the desert before them. "I've taken care of everything."

Sounding very unconvinced, Han said, "Oh . . . great!"

On the barge, Jabba pulled hard this time at the chain that bound Leia, yanking her away from the window and up against his side. She tried to pull away, but Bib Fortuna moved in behind her and pressed his long-fingered hand against her bare back, pushing her against the drooling Hutt. Jabba raised a goblet to Leia and drunkenly burbled in Huttese, "Soon you will learn to appreciate me."

C-3PO was also traveling on the barge. As he made his way past a group of intoxicated aliens, he bumped into a shorter droid who was carrying a tray of drinks. The tray and goblets clattered to the floor, and the droid immediately let out a series of angry beeps and whistles. Looking down, C-3PO said, "Oh, I'm terribly sor — Artoo! What are you doing here?"

R2-D2 thought his appearance spoke for itself, but the astromech beeped a quick reply.

"Well, I can see you're serving drinks," C-3PO said. "But this place is dangerous. They're going to execute Master Luke and, if we're not careful, us, too!"

Unconcerned, R2-D2 whistled a singsong response.

"Hmm," C-3PO said. "I wish I had your confidence."

The barge and skiffs arrived at the Great Pit of Carkoon, which was a huge sand basin. While the escort skiff circled the perimeter, the sail barge came to a hovering stop above the rim at one side of the depression. The prisoners' skiff stopped in the air above the pit's center.

Luke peered down over the skiff's railing and saw

a mucous-lined hole — just over two meters in diameter — at the bottom of the deep cone of sand. The hole was actually a mouth, and the mouth belonged to the Sarlacc, an omnivorous subterrestrial monster. Staggered rows of inward-pointing needle-shaped teeth ringed the mouth's upper area, and long tentacles stretched outward, trying to snag the skiff. A long appendage emerged from the mouth, rising like an angry serpent; at the end of this appendage was a sharp beaked mouth that snapped and bit at the dusty air.

A long, narrow metal plank was extended from the edge of the prisoners' skiff. The spear-wielding guards then released Luke's bonds and shoved him onto the plank.

On the barge, Jabba kept Leia against his side as he gazed across the pit to the prisoners' skiff. At Jabba's urging, C-3PO picked up a bulky comlink that was hooked up to a loudspeaker. The golden droid's amplified voice announced, "Victims of the almighty Sarlacc: His Excellency hopes that you will die honorably. But should any of you wish to beg for mercy, the great Jabba the Hutt will now listen to your pleas."

As Jabba took the comlink from C-3PO, no one noticed R2-D2 heading for a nearby stairway that led to the upper deck. Clutching the comlink close to his mouth, Jabba laughed and said, "Jedi . . ."

Before Jabba could continue, Han shouted back, "Threepio, you tell that slimy piece of worm-ridden filth he'll get no such pleasure from us." Han glanced at Chewbacca and added, "Right?"

Chewbacca growled in agreement.

Luke saw R2-D2 roll out onto the barge's exposed upper deck. The droid had shed the heavy tray of drinks and took his position beside the railing that overlooked the Sarlacc pit.

"Jabba!" Luke called out. "This is your last chance. Free us or die."

Hearing this seemingly ludicrous threat, Jabba and his motley companions were almost overcome by their own mocking laughter. Because Jabba was holding the comlink right up to his mouth, the barge's loudspeakers made his laughter rumble over the area. When the hysteria subsided, Jabba said in Huttese, "Move him into position."

A guard prodded Luke to the edge of the plank until he stood almost directly above the Sarlacc's gaping maw. Luke looked to Lando and nodded. Lando nodded back.

Luke lifted his gaze to R2-D2 on the barge's deck, then gave the droid a jaunty salute. It was the signal R2-D2 had been waiting for. A panel slid back from the astromech's domed head, revealing Luke's concealed lightsaber. Luke's original lightsaber had been lost during his duel with Darth Vader on Cloud

City, but he'd constructed a new one on Tatooine. He'd already used it, and knew that it worked.

Oblivious to the silent exchange between Luke and R2-D2, Jabba faced the prisoners' skiff and commanded in Huttese, "Put him in."

At that moment, Luke jumped off the plank and turned, catching the end of the plank by his fingertips. The plank bent down with Luke's weight, then sprang back up, catapulting him skyward.

R2-D2 simultaneously launched the lightsaber from his dome. As the weapon arced up and away from the barge, Luke executed a midair somersault and landed on the skiff beside Han and Chewbacca. He casually extended his left arm, and the lightsaber landed in his waiting palm.

Luke instantly ignited the lightsaber and attacked the two guards behind Han and Chewbacca. At the skiff's stern, Lando tore off his own helmet and swung it hard at the pilot behind the controls. Luke's lightsaber flashed furiously — two guards dropped their weapons as they toppled overboard, screaming as they slid down the pit's sandy slope into the Sarlacc's mouth.

Jabba exploded with rage and Leia trembled. The Hutt ordered the guards around him to go to their battle stations, and the guards went running. As a Gamorrean knocked C-3PO to the floor, Boba Fett raced for the stairway to the upper deck.

Luke swung his lightsaber again and sent two more guards into the deadly pit. Stepping over a spear and a blaster pistol that had fallen to the skiff's deck, he hurried to untie the bonds on Chewbacca's wrists. The Wookiee barked anxiously. Luke said, "Easy, Chewie."

Lando was still struggling with the skiff pilot when some guards appeared on the barge's upper deck. Jabba had not anticipated trouble from Luke and his allies, so heavy canvas tarpaulin had been secured over the custom-mounted laser cannon to keep the weapon free of sand. While a pair of Gamorreans hastily removed the tarp, a flat-faced Nikto with multiple nostrils slapped a portable blaster cannon onto the deck's railing. The Nikto fired at the armored skiff, and the power of the blast sent both Lando and the pilot overboard.

A length of rope fell away from the side of the skiff, and Lando grabbed for it, then swung out, dangling over the pit. The pilot wasn't so lucky and plunged into the Sarlacc.

"Whoa!" Lando shouted, clinging to the rope. "Whoa! Help!"

On the barge's upper deck, Fett took two swift strides from an open hatch, fired the jets on his backpack, and blasted away from the barge. As Chewbacca untied Han's bonds, Fett flew over the pit, landed on the prisoners' skiff, and brought his blaster rifle up fast. But before he could fire, Luke spun with his lightsaber and hacked off the blaster's barrel.

The skiff was rocked by another blast from the Nikto on the barge. The impact sprayed shards of metal everywhere, and Chewbacca threw himself protectively in front of Han, knocking him to the deck.

"Chewie!" Han shouted. "You're hit?"

Rolling away from Han, Chewbacca clutched at his left leg and howled.

Han grabbed at the air and said, "Where is he?"

Concerned for his friends, Luke looked away from Boba Fett for just an instant, and the bounty hunter took full advantage of the distraction. He launched a strong metal cable from his wrist gauntlet, and the cable whipped rapidly around Luke, pinning his arms against his sides. But Luke was holding his lightsaber in his right hand, and his wrist was still free; bending it, he brought the lightsaber's blade straight up and sliced through the cable.

As the cable fell away from Luke, another blast struck the skiff, knocking Boba Fett to the deck. The bounty hunter remained motionless as Lando, still dangling below the skiff, shouted, "Han! Chewie!"

"Lando!" Han called back.

Just then, laserfire from a different direction whizzed past Luke's head. He turned to see it came from the blaster-wielding guards on the escort skiff, which had swung in over the Sarlacc pit. Thinking Fett was disabled and that Han and Chewbacca could take care of Lando, Luke sprang through the air to land on the other skiff.

As Luke swung his lightsaber, Chewbacca barked at Han, directing him to pick up a dropped spear. Then Chewbacca saw Boba Fett, who was badly shaken, pushing himself up from the deck. The Wookiee barked desperately to Han.

"Boba Fett?!" Han answered, startled, as he picked up the spear.

Fett saw Luke fighting on the neighboring skiff. Using his right arm to steady his left, the dazed bounty hunter raised his wrist gauntlet and aimed at Luke. Fett fired, but the shot went high. Behind him, Han repeated, "Boba Fett?! Where?" He turned blindly, swinging the spear hard.

By sheer luck, the spear whacked the middle of the bounty hunter's backpack. The impact caused the jetpack to ignite, and Fett was launched from the skiff like a missile. His flight sent him smashing against the side of the sail barge, then he fell back, tumbling to the pit below. The weight of his armor and pack caused him to slide that much faster down the pit's slope and into the Sarlacc's mouth. A moment later, the Sarlacc burped loudly.

Jabba was so stunned by the sight of Boba Fett's

apparent demise that he finally dropped his bulky comlink. Leia snatched it up and brought it down hard upon an instrument panel that housed the barge's power circuits. All the shuttered windows slammed shut at the same time as the lights went out.

Leia leaped up behind Jabba, draping her chain over his head and around his bulbous neck. Hanging on to the chain, she then threw herself backward, letting her weight pull the chain taut against his throat. She put her muscle into it and twisted the chain hard. The Hutt's flaccid neck contracted under the tightening chain, and his eyes bulged out from their sockets.

Leia kept on tugging with all her might. *Now you know how it feels to have cold iron around your throat, Jabba!*

The Hutt's tail twitched, then his scum-coated tongue flopped out of his head.

He was dead.

Outside the barge, Luke continued to fight the guards on the escort skiff while Han extended his spear down to Lando's dangling form below the other skiff. Stretching the spear out as far as he could, Han said, "Lando, grab it!"

"Lower it!" Lando said as Luke sent more guards into the pit.

"I'm trying!" Han replied.

The Nikto fired again from the barge and an explosive blast struck the skiff, knocking the repulsorlift craft on its side. Although the skiff's steering vanes dug into the sand and prevented the craft from sliding into the pit, virtually everything on deck — including Han, Chewbacca, and a few scattered weapons — started to slide overboard. The rope snapped, and Lando fell to the sandy slope above the Sarlacc's open mouth, but he dug his heels into the sand and managed to stop his descent.

One of Han's feet snagged the skiff railing and he found himself dangling upside down above Lando and the pit. "Whoa! Whoa! Whoa!" Han shouted. Above him, the wounded Chewbacca hung on to the skiff for dear life. Han called, "Grab me, Chewie! I'm slipping!"

The Wookiee grabbed Han's feet, and Han extended the spear again toward Lando, who was clutching at the side of the pit, trying to dig a handhold. On the other skiff, Luke had dispensed with the last guard when he looked up to see more armed thugs running out onto the barge's deck, where the Gamorreans had finally removed the tarp from the laser cannon. As the figures on the barge fired at his friends, Luke leaped from the skiff to the bare-metal side of the sail barge. His body slammed against the hull but he caught hold of the edges of a closed window.

Suddenly, a hatch opened to his left and a leathery-skinned Weequay popped out, holding a menacing blaster pistol. Luke reached over, grabbed the Weequay's wrist, and yanked him straight out of the hatch. The alien yelled as he fell past Lando to the waiting Sarlacc, who hadn't eaten so well in a long time.

Lando lay motionless to avoid slipping further. Above him, Chewbacca continued to cling to the upside-down Han, who extended the spear again to Lando and said, "Grab it!" Lando reached carefully. Han said, "Almost . . . you almost got it!"

But the Nikto and other gunners fired yet again from the barge, striking the front of the tilted skiff and causing Lando to let go of the spear. Lando shouted, "Hold it! Whoa!"

The gunners were about to release another barrage when Luke leaped onto the barge's deck. He activated his lightsaber and made quick work of the Nikto, then moved fast toward the other guards, alternately cutting down their weapons and deflecting fired laserbolts back at the shooters.

Han extended the spear to Lando again. "Gently now," Han said. "All . . . all right. Easy. Hold me, Chewie."

Lando screamed. One of the Sarlacc's tentacles had coiled itself tightly around his ankle and was dragging him down.

Hanging onto the spear, Han glanced up and

hazily saw the barrel of a guard's fallen blaster sticking out from the skiff. "Chewie!" Han shouted. "Chewie, give me the gun." The Wookiee passed the blaster down to Han's free hand. Han said, "Don't move, Lando."

"No, wait!" Lando cried. "I thought you were blind!"

"It's all right," Han said. "Trust me. Don't move."

Lando saw that Han, still fuzzy-eyed, was unintentionally aiming the blaster's barrel at Lando's legs. "A little higher!" Lando shouted. "Just a little higher!"

Han adjusted his aim and fired. The laserbolt struck the tentacle, and the Sarlacc let out a pained shriek as it released Lando, who grabbed the spear and held tight.

"Chewie, pull us up!" Han shouted. "All right . . . up, Chewie, up!"

Chewbacca began pulling Han up, but his muscles were strained. Fortunately, Lando was able to work his way up the steep slope, and he climbed back onto the skiff to help the Wookiee.

During all this commotion, R2-D2 had managed to avoid being hit or trampled and had returned to the banquet room to find Leia still chained to Jabba's corpse. From his cylindrical body, R2-D2 readily deployed and extended his laser torch, then fired a controlled burst at the chain, neatly cutting it and freeing Leia.

"Come on," Leia said to R2-D2. "We gotta get out of here."

As they raced for the exit, R2-D2 found C-3PO lying on the floor, kicking and screaming. Salacious Crumb was on top of him and had pulled the droid's right photoreceptor straight out of his eye socket.

"Not my eyes!" C-3PO yelled. "Artoo, help! Quickly, Artoo. Oh! Ohhh!"

Deploying his laser torch again, R2-D2 bravely raced over and zapped Salacious Crumb. The monkey-lizard screamed and leaped to the upper rafters.

"Beast!" C-3PO exclaimed before he hurried after R2-D2, heading for the hatch to the upper deck.

Leia was already there. She stepped out of the hatch to find Luke engaged in combat with several guards. Swinging his lightsaber, Luke warded off laserbolts and fought fiercely. He caught sight of Leia and said, "Get the gun! Point it at the deck!"

Leia turned to the large laser cannon. Following Luke's instructions, she stepped over the removed tarp and climbed up onto the weapon's turret platform. As she began to swivel the cannon around, Luke raised his lightsaber to fend off another attacker and repeated, "Point it at the deck!"

A guard fired at Luke and the blast hit the back of his mechanical hand. His hand was sensory wired, and Luke groaned at the sudden stab of pain. Maintaining his grip on the lightsaber, Luke pushed the pain from his mind and lashed out to dispose of the guard who'd shot him.

Across the deck, R2-D2 beeped wildly, urging C-3PO to head for a gap between the railings on the barge's starboard side, which overlooked a sandy dune. His vision still impaired from his encounter with Salacious Crumb, the golden droid said, "Artoo, where are we going? I couldn't possibly jump . . ."

R2-D2 butted C-3PO, sending him over the edge to land headfirst in the sand below. Without hesitation, R2-D2 boldly stepped off and landed beside his friend.

Luke ran along the empty deck toward Leia and the laser cannon, which was now pointed at the deck. Luke grabbed hold of a rigging rope from one of the barge's masts, then looked to Leia and said, "Come on!"

Leia ran to Luke. He tightened his grip on the rope and wrapped an arm around Leia's waist, then kicked the trigger of the laser cannon. The cannon fired into the deck as Luke and Leia swung out from the barge. Sweeping over the sand pit, they landed on the skiff beside Han, who was treating Chewbacca's wounded leg.

Lando was at the skiff's controls. Luke said, "Let's go! And don't forget the droids."

"We're on our way," Lando said with a winning smile.

A loud explosion rocked the sail barge, as Lando guided the skiff around to the barge's starboard side, where they saw R2-D2's periscope and C-3PO's legs sticking out of the sand. Lando hastily deployed two large electromagnets from the bottom of the skiff and hoisted both droids up from the dune just before a greater explosion tore through the barge.

A chain of explosions followed. As the skiff sped off across the desert, heading for the *Millennium Falcon* and Luke's X-wing starfighter, Jabba's sail barge settled into the sand and disappeared in one final conflagration.

CHAPTER 5

Imperial Star Destroyers were among the ships in the blockade orbiting Tatooine. The blockade had been in place since Darth Vader had failed to capture Luke Skywalker at Bespin. It hadn't been easy for Luke's X-wing and the *Millennium Falcon* to avoid the blockade when they'd traveled to Tatooine to rescue Han Solo, but getting off had been relatively simple, thanks to R2-D2.

While on Jabba's barge, the astromech droid had penetrated the Hutt's data system, and alerted the goons who'd remained in Jabba's palace that the Imperials were coming for them with death warrants. The Imperial ships could hardly ignore the flotilla of smuggler ships, corsair gunboats, and slave transports that lifted off from the Hutt's compound en masse; and in the battle that followed, they failed to notice the single X-wing starfighter and Corellian freighter that rose away from Tatooine by a more discreet route.

Luke was piloting his X-wing and R2-D2 was plugged into the astromech socket behind the cockpit. Han was once again behind the controls of the *Falcon*, which he'd won from Lando Calrissian in a game of sabacc some years back. After leaving Tatooine behind, the two ships veered off in different directions across space.

"Meet you back at the fleet," Luke said into his cockpit's comlink.

"Hurry," Leia answered from the *Falcon*. "The Alliance should be assembled by now."

"I will," Luke said.

Then Han broke in: "Hey, Luke, thanks. Thanks for comin' after me. Now I owe you one."

Luke smiled, then angled his ship for a distant star. Behind him, R2-D2 beeped, and Luke glanced at one of his scopes to read the droid's message. Luke replied, "That's right, Artoo. We're going to the Dagobah system. I have a promise to keep . . . to an old friend."

R2-D2 had previously accompanied Luke to Dagobah, so the droid knew Luke was referring to the Jedi Master Yoda. The artificial skin on the back of Luke's right hand had been blasted away by the hit he'd taken on Jabba's sail barge. He pulled a black leather glove over his damaged hand and thought, *Why did Ben tell me Darth Vader killed my father? Does Yoda know the truth? If he does, why didn't he tell me?*

Or . . . is it possible that Ben did tell me the truth, and that Vader was trying to deceive me?

Filled with uncertainty, Luke plotted the course to the Dagobah system, then made the jump into hyperspace.

In a great display of the Empire's might, a parade of thousands of TIE fighters traveled in orbit of the Death Star to mark the arrival of Emperor Palpatine. Like Darth Vader, the Emperor traveled in a *Lambda*-class shuttle. Vader stood in a large docking bay and watched the three-winged spacecraft approach his position.

He was not alone. The docking bay was filled nearly to capacity with Imperial troops in tight formation. Commander Jerjerrod, the beleaguered officer in charge of the Death Star's construction, stood near Vader and tried not to tremble. Glancing at the black-helmeted dark lord of the Sith, Jerjerrod wondered if Darth Vader had ever been anxious about anything in his entire life, then dismissed the thought as ridiculous.

In fact, Vader was feeling uneasy. Not about the Emperor's arrival, but about finding Luke Skywalker. *Luke defeated me at the first Death Star. He evaded me on Hoth, and escaped at Bespin. I cannot lose him again. The longer I remain on this space station, the more he exceeds my reach.*

The shuttle entered the docking bay and landed on its gleaming black deck. The landing ramp descended and Vader watched six Royal Guards disembark; handpicked for their fighting prowess and loyalty to the Emperor, all wore blood red helmets and robes, and carried two-meter-long pikes. After the Royal Guards took their positions at the base of the landing ramp, the Emperor himself emerged. Darth Vader and Commander Jerjerrod genuflected.

Hunched and walking with a gnarled cane, Emperor Palpatine's ghastly, withered features were barely visible under the hood of his heavy black cloak. He was followed down the landing ramp by several Imperial dignitaries. Stopping before Vader's kneeling form, the Emperor said, "Rise, my friend."

Vader rose to walk alongside the Emperor, who moved slowly past the long rows of troops.

"The Death Star will be completed on schedule," Vader reported.

"You have done well, Lord Vader," the Emperor replied, his voice a decrepit rasp. "And now I sense you wish to continue your search for young Skywalker."

"Yes, my Master."

"Patience, my friend. In time, he will seek you out. And when he does, you must bring him before *me*. He has grown *strong*. Only together can we turn him to the dark side of the Force."

For a thousand years, the Sith had maintained their order by never having more than two Sith Lords: a Master and a single apprentice. The few attempts to expand their number beyond two had always led to the Sith Lords conspiring to kill each other. Vader did not question why the Emperor dared to challenge the long tradition. He said, "As you wish."

The Emperor leered and said, "Everything is proceeding as I have foreseen." Then he cackled to himself, and the evil sound echoed across the docking bay.

Luke's arrival on Dagobah went much smoother than it had on his first visit, when his inexperience with navigating the swamp world's dense mists and towering trees had led to a crash landing. Now, his X-wing rested on a muddy knoll, just a short distance from Yoda's small cottage.

R2-D2 stood beside the starfighter and beeped disconsolately to himself; he didn't like to complain, but he found nothing appealing about Dagobah's climate, terrain, or wildlife. The tightly clustered trees were so thick with foliage that sunlight rarely reached the rainforest's floor, and it sounded like there were creatures lurking everywhere. R2-D2 looked to Yoda's house, a mud-packed structure that was partially framed by the roots of a massive tree.

The droid saw warm golden light in the oddly shaped windows, and wondered how long he and Luke would stay this time.

Inside the low-ceilinged structure, Luke sat and watched Yoda move to warm himself beside the flaming scraps of deadwood in the fireplace. Luke couldn't help but notice that the aged Jedi Master moved more slowly and carefully, and was more dependent on the twisted gimer stick he used to steady himself. It was hard for Luke to imagine Yoda using the stick to playfully whack R2-D2 as he had in the past. *He's aged so much since I last saw him.*

Yoda turned his wrinkled green head to gaze at Luke's concerned expression. "Hmm. That face you make? Look I so old to young eyes?"

"No . . . of course not," Luke said, offering a feeble smile.

"I do, yes, I do!" Yoda said. "Sick have I become. Old and weak." Pointing a crooked finger at his guest, he added, "When nine hundred years old you reach, look as good you will not. Hmm?" He chuckled to himself at this, then hobbled slowly across the room, each movement a struggle, and climbed onto his small bed. "Soon will I rest. Yes, forever sleep. Earned it, I have." He was so weak, he could barely manage to pull his blanket up over himself.

Luke moved beside the bed to help cover the aged Jedi. He said, "Master Yoda, you can't die."

"Strong am I with the Force . . . but not that strong! Twilight is upon me, and soon night must fall. That is the way of things . . . the way of the Force."

"But I need your help. I've come back to complete the training."

"No more training do you require. Already know you that which you need," Yoda sighed and settled back against his pillow.

Luke looked away. "Then I *am* a Jedi."

"Ohhh," Yoda said, then shook his head. "Not yet. One thing remains: Vader. You must confront Vader. Then, only then, a Jedi will you be. And confront him you will."

Luke was silent for a moment, trying to build up the courage to ask the question that had plagued him since his duel with Darth Vader on Cloud City. *I have to ask. I must know the truth!*

"Master Yoda . . . is Darth Vader my father?"

Yoda's eyes were full of weariness. A sad smile creased his face, then he turned painfully on his side, so he was facing away from Luke. "Mmm . . . rest I need," he muttered. "Yes . . . rest."

Luke looked at the back of Yoda's head. *Why won't he tell me? Why?*

"Yoda, I must know," he insisted.

Yoda sighed and finally said, "Your father he is. Told you, did he?"

"Yes."

Yoda's brow furrowed and he frowned with concern. "Unexpected this is," he said, "and unfortunate . . ."

"Unfortunate that I know the truth?"

"No," Yoda said. Gathering his strength, he turned over again so he could look at Luke. "Unfortunate that you rushed to face him . . . that incomplete was your training. That not ready for the burden were you."

"I'm sorry," Luke said.

"Remember, a Jedi's strength flows from the Force. But beware. Anger, fear, aggression. The dark side are they. Once you start down the dark path, forever will it dominate your destiny." Yoda's breathing had become strained, his voice a faint gasping whisper. "Luke . . . Luke . . ."

Luke moved closer to Yoda. In the nearby fireplace, the burning wood crackled.

Yoda said, "Do not . . . do not underestimate the powers of the Emperor or suffer your father's fate, you will. Luke, when gone am I . . . the last of the Jedi will you be. Luke, the Force runs strong in your family. Pass on what you have learned, Luke . . ." Yoda closed his eyes. With great effort, he spoke his last words: "There is . . . another . . . Sky . . . walker."

Luke was stunned. *Another Skywalker?! But who? And where?*

Yoda caught his breath, then his facial muscles relaxed and all his breath left him. Luke stared at Yoda's body. He simply could not believe that the Jedi Master was gone. *Come back. Without your help, I'll fail. Don't go.*

To Luke's amazement, Yoda's body then began to fade . . . until it had completely disappeared, leaving an empty space between the bed and blankets. From outside the mud-packed house came the sound of distant thunder. The blankets slowly collapsed upon the bed.

Luke was stunned. He'd already lost so many friends and loved ones that he'd wondered if the loss of one more would even hurt. Now he had his answer: The pain was tremendous. And all that was left of Yoda were his few belongings and Luke's memories.

Luke looked away from the empty bed, then looked back at it. He wasn't sure what to do. Ducking under the low ceiling, he moved away from the bed and headed for the door, leaving the fire burning in the fireplace.

Emerging from Yoda's home, Luke wandered back to his X-wing. He'd never felt so alone and apart from others, so lost and far away.

Luke and R2-D2 prepared to leave Dagobah. R2-D2 was under the X-wing, using his extendable torch to make a minor repair to the ship's lower starboard thrust engine. Luke looked to the windows of

Yoda's house just as the firelight flickered and died. The windows went dark.

The droid beeped to Luke, but he remained silent, thinking. *Perhaps Yoda and Ben were right when they warned me not to try rescuing my friends on Cloud City. I didn't rescue anyone. The only useful thing I did was travel to Bespin with Artoo; if he hadn't wound up fixing the* Millennium Falcon's *hyperdrive, everyone on board might have been captured by Vader.*

Good ol' Artoo.

Luke knelt beside the astromech to inspect his work. Reaching up to touch the X-wing's repaired engine, Luke realized he was still wearing the black glove that concealed his damaged mechanical hand.

Yoda and Ben were also right about Darth Vader. I wasn't ready to confront him then. But without Yoda, how will I truly know I'm ready?

Luke lowered his hand. "I can't do it, Artoo," he said, shaking his head. He rose to stand beside the droid. "I can't go on alone."

Unexpectedly, from a nearby grove of trees, came a familiar voice: "Yoda will always be with you."

Luke turned. "Obi-Wan!"

And there he was: Obi-Wan Kenobi. Old Ben. More precisely, a shimmering semi-transparent apparition of Ben. He moved out from behind some nearby trees to stand facing Luke.

Approaching Ben's spirit, Luke asked, "Why didn't you tell me? You told me Vader betrayed and murdered my father."

"Your father was seduced by the dark side of the Force," Ben answered. "He ceased to be Anakin Skywalker and became Darth Vader. When that happened, the good man who was your father was destroyed. So what I told was true . . . from a certain point of view."

"A certain point of view!" Luke repeated derisively.

"Luke, you're going to find that many of the truths we cling to depend greatly on our own point of view." Ben's spirit eased himself down to sit upon the length of a fallen tree. "Anakin was a good friend."

Luke realized Ben really did think of Anakin Skywalker and Darth Vader as two separate people. Listening, he sat beside Ben, who continued, "When I first knew him, your father was already a great pilot. But I was amazed how strongly the Force was with him. I took it upon myself to train him as a Jedi. I thought that I could instruct him just as well as Yoda. I was wrong."

"There is still good in him," Luke said, not just hopefully, but as if he knew it to be true.

Ben believed just the opposite: that Anakin was dead, and Vader was beyond salvation. "He's more machine now than man," he said. "Twisted and evil."

Luke shook his head. "I can't do it, Ben."

Ben's gaze flicked to Luke. "You cannot escape your destiny. You must face Darth Vader again."

"I can't kill my own father."

Ben looked away. "Then the Emperor has already won," he said with a sigh. "You were our only hope."

Maybe not, Luke thought. He said, "Yoda spoke of another."

Ben returned his gaze to Luke, studying him, trying to decide whether the young man was ready for another revelation, or if it were best for everyone if Luke remained ignorant. Ben made a decision, and said, "The other he spoke of is your twin sister."

Bewildered, Luke said, "But I have no sister."

"To protect you both from the Emperor, you were hidden from your father when you were born. The Emperor knew, as I did, if Anakin were to have any offspring, they would be a threat to him. That is the reason why your sister remains safely anonymous."

Incredibly, Luke was suddenly aware of his sister's identity. "Leia! Leia's my sister."

"Your insight serves you well," Ben said. "Bury your feelings deep down, Luke. They do you credit. But they could be made to serve the Emperor."

Luke nodded, agreeing with Ben. *Yes . . . I must bury my feelings. If the Emperor learned about Leia, he'd want her, too.*

But what about my father? What would he do if he knew Leia were his daughter?

Luke looked into the distance, as if he might catch some glimpse of what the future held. But all he saw was a heavy mist flowing over the swamp and past the trees. He glanced back to the figure that had been sitting beside him, but Ben was gone.

CHAPTER 6

The planet Sullust was a volcanic world in the Outer Rim Territories. It had a highly toxic atmosphere, but beneath its rocky surface lived millions of humanoid Sullustans. They had jowled faces with wide, black-orbed eyes and large ears, and their technologically advanced subterranean cities were highly regarded for their beauty. Sullust was also home to SoroSuub, a prominent corporation that manufactured star-ships, weapons, and droids. Because an influential SoroSuub executive remained grateful to the Alliance for rescuing him from Imperial captivity, the Rebel fleet had been allowed to rendezvous in the Sullust system.

The vast Rebel fleet included several small Corellian battleships, many single-pilot starfighters, a few Gallofree Yards Medium transports, and a Nebulon-B frigate that had been converted for medical duty. The blimp-shaped Mon Calamari Star Cruisers were the largest and most unusual-looking ships, their fluid exteriors covered by bulging protuberances that gave the vessels an organic quality, as if they'd been grown, not built.

One of the Mon Cal cruisers, the 1,200-meter-long *Home One*, had been originally designed as a peaceful exploration ship; refitted with recessed weapons batteries and shield generators, it was now the personal flagship for Admiral Ackbar. Like other Mon Calamari, Ackbar was an amphibian with salmon-colored skin, large, bulbous yellow-orange eyes, and webbed hands and feet.

Ackbar stood with his Mon Calamari officers in a holographic ampitheater that had been transformed into a briefing room. Staggered rows of white plastoid seats encircled a central console unit that resembled a wheel lying on the floor; the console housed a retracted holographic projector. Ackbar watched the military leaders and a few dozen pilots file into the ampitheater and take their seats.

Princess Leia, Han Solo, Chewbacca, and C-3PO were present, as was the X-wing pilot Wedge Antilles. Among the other pilots were several aliens, including a Sullustan named Nien Nunb. Thanks to Chewbacca, C-3PO's right eye was repaired and the golden droid could again see clearly; he thought Leia looked splendid in her Alliance-issue uniform.

As Chewbacca took a seat, Han spotted Lando,

who was wearing a floor-length dress cape with an impeccably tailored Alliance uniform. Glancing at the rank plaque on Lando's tunic, Han said, "Well, look at you, a general, huh?"

Lando grinned. "Someone must have told them about my little maneuver at the Battle of Taanab."

Han knew all about Lando's skirmish with the notorious Norulac space pirates in the Taanab system. Han said sarcastically, "Well, don't look at me, pal. I just said you were a fair pilot. I didn't know they were lookin' for somebody to lead this crazy attack."

"I'm surprised they didn't ask you to do it."

"Well, who says they didn't?" Han asked. "But I ain't crazy. You're the respectable one, remember?" Han took a seat beside Chewbacca. Lando smiled broadly.

As Leia sat down beside Han, a human woman in a white gown entered the room. She had auburn hair and pale blue-green eyes, and wore a gold medallion around her neck. As a young Senator from the planet Chandrila, she had been one of the founders of the Alliance to Restore the Republic. She was now the leader of the Rebellion. Her name was Mon Mothma.

An electronic chime sounded, signaling the audience for their attention. The room fell silent as Mon Mothma stepped beside the ampitheater's central console unit. "The Emperor has made a critical error," she announced, "and the time for our attack has come."

The ampitheater's lights dimmed and Mon Mothma looked to the middle of the console unit, where a holographic projector extended up. Above the projector, a light-generated three-dimensional image of a rotating green world appeared; the green hologram was orbited by a second hologram, a relatively smaller sphere that was an incomplete structure, colored red for visual clarity. From either personal experience or familiarity with the Battle at Yavin, everyone in the room recognized the smaller hologram as an unfinished Imperial Death Star.

"The data brought to us by the Bothan spies pinpoints the exact location of the Emperor's new battle station," Mon Mothma said. "We also know that the weapon systems of this Death Star are not yet operational. With the Imperial fleet spread throughout the galaxy in a vain effort to engage us, it is relatively unprotected. But most important of all, we've learned that the Emperor himself is personally overseeing the final stages of the construction of this Death Star." Mon Mothma swallowed hard. "Many Bothans died to bring us this information. Admiral Ackbar, please."

Admiral Ackbar stepped up beside the central console and gestured to the holograms. "You can see here the Death Star orbiting the forest moon of

Endor," Ackbar said in his gravelly voice. "Although the weapon systems on this Death Star are not yet operational, the Death Star does have a strong defense mechanism. It is protected by an energy shield, which is generated from the nearby forest moon of Endor."

From the "surface" of the green moon's hologram, a yellow stream of light — representing the energy shield — appeared to project and wrap around the Death Star. Ackbar continued, "The shield must be deactivated if any attack is to be attempted."

Every pilot in the room knew Ackbar's statement as a given fact. Planetary shields were so powerful that any starship unlucky enough to career into one were either severely damaged or instantly vaporized.

The hologram of the forest moon and energy shield vanished, and the Death Star's hologram rapidly magnified to fill the space above the central console. The enlarged image was a three-dimensional cross-section that displayed an internal route to the center of the incomplete space station. Ackbar said, "Once the shield is down, our cruisers will create a perimeter, while the fighters fly into the superstructure and attempt to knock out the main reactor. General Calrissian has volunteered to lead the fighter attack."

Surprised, Han turned to Lando with renewed respect and wished him luck. Then added, "You're gonna need it."

Admiral Ackbar stepped back and said, "General Madine."

A brown-bearded, middle-aged human, General Crix Madine had been a highly decorated Imperial officer before he'd defected to the Alliance. Madine stepped forward and announced, "We have stolen a small Imperial shuttle. Disguised as a cargo ship and using a secret Imperial code, a strike team will land on the moon and deactivate the shield generator."

Hearing this, the assembled group exchanged nervous glances and mumbled among themselves. C-3PO said, "Sounds dangerous."

Leia leaned closer to Han and said, "I wonder who they found to pull that off."

Scanning the ampitheater, Madine located Han's seated figure and said, "General Solo, is your strike team assembled?"

Leia, startled, turned to look at Han. Then her surprise changed to admiration.

"Uh, my team's ready," Han said, squirming under the attention that was suddenly given to him. "I don't have a command crew for the shuttle."

Beside Han, Chewbacca raised his hairy paw and barked, volunteering.

"Well, it's gonna be rough, pal," Han said. "I didn't want to speak for you."

Chewbacca growled cheerfully, conveying to everyone that the choice was his.

Han smiled. "That's one."

"Uh, General," Leia said, "count me in."

"I'm with you, too!" Luke volunteered as he entered the room from the rear. He'd just arrived from Dagobah with R2-D2, who wobbled over to talk with C-3PO. Making his way down to the ampitheater's floor, Luke arrived before Leia, who embraced him warmly. Then, sensing a change in him, she pulled away and looked into his eyes.

"What is it?" she asked.

Luke thought, *I still can't believe she's my sister.* But he couldn't tell her now. He hesitated, then said, "Ask me again sometime."

Han, Chewbacca, and Lando crowded around Luke as the assembly broke up.

"Luke," Han said, extending his hand.

Luke took it. "Hi, Han . . . Chewie." *It feels so good to be among friends again.*

R2-D2 beeped a singsong observation to C-3PO.

C-3PO shuddered and replied, "'Exciting' is hardly the word *I* would choose."

An Imperial shuttle, the *Tydirium* was twenty meters long and had a trihedral foil design: The tall dorsal stabilizer remained stationary but the two lower wings extended during flight and folded upward for landing. Before it had been transported to the Sullust System, the *Tydirium* had been captured by the Alliance with the help of "Ace" Azzameen at an orbital outpost at Zhar. Now, looking very out of place, the Imperial shuttle rested beside the *Millennium Falcon* and several single-pilot starfighters in the main docking bay of Admiral Ackbar's Mon Cal cruiser.

Han and Lando stood between the *Falcon* and the *Tydirium*. As the Rebel strike team loaded weapons and supplies onto the shuttle, Han gestured to the *Falcon* and said, "Look: I *want* you to take her. I mean it. Take her. You need all the help you can get. She's the fastest ship in the fleet."

"All right, old buddy," Lando said. "You know, I know what she means to you. I'll take good care of her. She — she won't get a scratch. All right?"

"Right," Han said. He turned for the shuttle, then stopped and looked back to Lando. "I got your promise. Not a scratch."

"Look, would you get going, you pirate." Lando exchanged salutes with Han, then added, "Good luck."

"You, too," Han said, and headed up the shuttle's ramp.

Inside, he saw Leia briefing the twelve SpecForces Rebel commandos seated in the shuttle's aft area. The commandos wore combat uniforms of full forest-camouflage fatigues, and their unit leader was Major Bren Derlin. Han had worked with Derlin and his SpecForces soldiers on Hoth and knew they had what it took to get the difficult job done. Like the commandos, Leia wore a camouflage poncho.

There were three seats on each side of the *Tydirium*'s cockpit. C-3PO sat in the rear portside seat and R2-D2 stood close by. In front of C-3PO, Luke — also wearing a camouflage poncho — was adjusting switches on a control panel. At fore starboard, Chewbacca was in the co-pilot's seat.

Han moved past the droids and Luke and stepped down to the pilot's seat. Beside him, Chewbacca was having a hard time figuring out all the Imperial controls.

"You got her warmed?" Han asked Luke.

"Yeah, she's comin' up," Luke replied with confidence.

Chewbacca growled a complaint about the controls.

Han answered, "I don't think the Empire had Wookiees in mind when they designed her, Chewie." As the shuttle warmed up, Han looked out the window to the *Millennium Falcon*, which was just across the docking bay . . . but somehow seemed impossibly out of reach.

Han felt a chill run up his spine.

Leia entered the cockpit and placed a hand on his shoulder. He flinched and glanced at her.

"Hey," Leia said, "are you awake?"

"Yeah," Han said sadly, returning his gaze to the *Falcon*. "I just got a funny feeling. Like I'm not gonna see her again."

Speaking softly, Leia said, "Come on, General, let's move."

Han snapped back to life. "Right. Chewie."

Chewbacca roared, eager to get going. Leia took the seat behind Chewbacca.

Han said. "Let's see what this piece of junk can do. Ready, everybody?"

"All set," Luke said.

At the back of the cockpit, R2-D2 beeped.

C-3PO said, "Here we go again."

The *Tydirium* glided out of the docking bay and into space. Moving away from the Mon Cal cruiser, the shuttle's lower wings dropped to their extended position. Han steered the shuttle past the surrounding ships, then said, "All right, hang on." He threw a switch, and the *Tydirium* launched into hyperspace, on course for the Endor system.

In orbit of Endor's forest moon, the Death Star's construction continued. A formation of Imperial TIE fighters patrolled the space station's north pole, sweeping past a highly shielded tower that rose one hundred stories above the surface. The tower was topped by a control post that had been converted into a throne room and private observation chamber for Emperor Palpatine.

The Emperor's throne was a large, contoured chair with control panels in the arms; the chair rested on an elevated platform below a tall, circular window with radiating panes. A stairway extended down from the platform to the turbolifts and observation gallery. Except for the brightly colored instrument lights that ringed a pair of duty posts near the stairway, everything was black and dark gray, cold and metallic.

Standing beside his throne, Palpatine gazed out the window and surveyed the half-completed Death Star and Endor's moon. Behind him, members of the Imperial council watched silently as Darth Vader exited the turbolift on the other side of the chamber. Vader crossed a short bridge that extended over the tower's vast elevator shaft, then ascended the stairs to the upper platform.

Vader had been informed that a fleet of Rebel ships had assembled in the Sullust system, and suspected the Emperor wished to do something about it. Ignoring the Imperial dignitaries, Vader arrived before the Emperor and said, "What is thy bidding, my Master?"

Turning away from the window to face Vader, the Emperor replied, "Send the fleet to the far side of Endor. There it will stay until called for."

Vader said, "What of the reports of the Rebel fleet massing near Sullust?"

"It is of no concern," the Emperor assured him. "Soon the Rebellion will be crushed and young Skywalker will be one of us! Your work here is finished, my friend. Go out to the command ship and await my orders."

Vader bowed deeply and said, "Yes, my Master."

CHAPTER 7

The shuttle *Tydirium* dropped out of hyperspace and into the Endor system. The sight of a *Super*-class Star Destroyer, two *Imperial*-class Star Destroyers, and the half-finished Death Star would have been enough for most pilots to turn and run, but Han Solo's hands remained steady on the controls as he guided the shuttle toward the immense space station.

Han said, "If they don't go for this, we're gonna have to get outta here pretty quick, Chewie."

Sitting beside Han, Chewbacca growled in agreement.

From the shuttle's comlink came the voice of an Imperial controller: "We have you on our screen now. Please identify."

Han said, "Shuttle *Tydirium* requesting deactivation of the deflector shield."

The controller answered, "Shuttle *Tydirium*, transmit the clearance code for shield passage."

"Transmission commencing," Han said, and sent the code.

Leia and Luke were still seated behind Chewbacca and Han. In a hushed voice, Leia said, "Now we find out if that code is worth the price we paid."

"It'll work. It'll work," Han said reassuringly.

Chewbacca whined nervously. As they listened to the sound of the high-speed transmission from the shuttle's comm console, Luke stared at the Super Star Destroyer that was alongside the Death Star, orbiting Endor's moon.

"Vader's on that ship," Luke said.

"Now don't get jittery, Luke," Han told him. "There are a lot of command ships. Keep your distance, though, Chewie, but don't look like you're trying to keep your distance."

Wondering how he should accomplish this tactic, Chewbacca barked a question to Han.

"I don't know," Han replied. "Fly casual."

Luke is on that ship, Darth Vader thought to himself. He was standing before the wide viewport on the *Executor*'s main bridge as the shuttle glided by.

Vader turned from the viewport. He strode up the elevated command walkway that extended above the lower-level crew pits and moved toward Admiral Piett, the *Executor*'s commander. Wearing a gray uniform and cap, Piett had been looking over a black-uniformed controller's tracking screen when he noticed Vader's approach.

"Where is that shuttle going?" Vader asked.

Piett leaned over the controller's shoulder and spoke into the computer console's comlink: "Shuttle *Tydirium*, what is your cargo and destination?"

"Parts and technical crew for the forest moon," answered the filtered voice of the *Tydirium*'s pilot.

Piett looked to Vader, waiting for his reaction. Vader said, "Do they have code clearance?"

"It's an older code, sir," Piett said, "but it checks out. I was about to clear them."

Vader looked upward. *My son is so close. So very, very close.*

In the *Tydirium*'s cockpit, Luke was suddenly filled with trepidation. Although Vader had not communicated with him telepathically, as he had before Luke's escape at Bespin, Luke sensed that Vader was aware of his proximity. "I'm endangering the mission," Luke said. "I shouldn't have come."

"It's your imagination, kid," Han said. Glancing back, he saw that Leia appeared nervous, too. "Come on," Han continued. "Let's keep a little optimism here."

Chewbacca was still doing his best to "fly casual," but he let out an anxious growl.

*　　　*　　　*

On the *Executor's* bridge, Piett was starting to wonder about Vader's interest in the shuttle. "Shall I hold them?" he asked.

"No," Vader answered firmly. "Leave them to me. I will deal with them myself."

"As you wish, my lord," Piett said. To the controller, he commanded, "Carry on."

As Han Solo waited for a response from the *Executor*, he started to feel as uneasy as everyone else in the cockpit. There was practically no chance for the *Tydirium* to escape the area; all the Imperials had to do was aim a tractor beam at the stolen shuttle and the mission to Endor was over. Han gulped and said, "They're not goin' for it, Chewie."

Then the Imperial controller's voice spoke from the comm: "Shuttle *Tydirium*, deactivation of the shield will commence immediately. Follow your present course."

In the *Tydirium's* cockpit, there was a collective sigh of relief from everyone but Luke, who remained tense. Chewbacca barked.

"Okay!" Han said, glancing back at his friends. "I told you it was gonna work. No problem." He steered the shuttle away from the *Executor*, past the Death Star, and down to the forest moon of Endor.

The moon's unspoiled surface was covered with woodlands, savannas, and mountains. The *Tydirium* traveled over an ancient forest, where trees rose a thousand meters into the sky. Intending to avoid unnecessary contact with Imperial troops, Han landed the shuttle in a clearing several kilometers from their target: the moon-based energy shield generator protecting the orbital Death Star.

The Rebels disembarked. Luke, Leia, and the commandos wore helmets that matched their camouflage outfits. Han opted against a helmet and insisted on staying in his own clothes but did select a forest-camouflage duster, a long-sleeved coat that concealed most of his form. Everyone carried blasters except for the droids and Luke, who maintained that a lightsaber was the only weapon that a Jedi needed.

Long shafts of sunlight stretched from the towering treetops to the forest floor, but the wide-trunked trees grew so close together that it was often difficult to get a clear view in any direction. Moving cautiously, Han led his friends and the twelve SpecForces commandos down a hill, away from the shuttle.

They soon arrived at an adjacent hill, and Han saw something ahead. He raised a hand, signaling the rest of the group to stop. All the soldiers dropped to a crouch, instantly blending in with the surrounding dense foliage. At the rear of the procession, C-3PO looked to R2-D2 and said, "Oh, I told you it was dangerous here."

Han, Leia, Luke, and Chewbacca peered over a

fallen moss-covered tree. Not far below their position, two white-armored Imperial scout troopers were on patrol, moving on foot. Unlike stormtroopers, the scouts were trained to an unusual degree of independence for Imperial personnel and wore lightweight body armor. Their distinctive helmets had enhanced macrobinocular viewplates and boosted comlink systems for long-range communication.

Luke noticed a pair of three-meter-long speeder bikes parked near the scout troopers. Repulsorlift vehicles with front-mounted, sharp-edged directional steering vanes, the speeder bikes hung suspended in the air just above the ground. Although the bikes were primarily used for reconnaissance, each was equipped with a ventral blaster cannon.

Leia asked, "Should we try and go around?"

"It'll take time," Luke said.

"This whole party'll be for nothing if they see us," Han pointed out. "Chewie and I will take care of this. You stay here."

Remembering Han's inclination to shoot first and ask questions later, Luke glared at his friend and stressed, "*Quietly.* There might be more of them out there."

Apparently surprised by Luke's concern, Han grinned confidently and said, "Hey . . . it's *me.*"

Blaster in hand, Han started off through the bushes

C-3PO and R2-D2 approach the palace of
Jabba the Hutt. Beware!

Anyone who wishes to meet with Jabba must first
get past Bib Fortuna.

Sy Snootles and the Max Rebo Band play merry
alien music.

Chewbacca is held captive by a mysterious
bounty hunter.

Han Solo—trapped in carbonized limbo.

Princess Leia Organa rescues Han . . .

. . . but who will rescue Leia?

Luke Skywalker—with new Jedi powers.

The rancor, a man-eating giant, seeks its next meal,

In the middle of the desert, Luke must find an escape.

A lightsaber is a handy weapon in a tight situation!

The galactic bounty hunter
Boba Fett battles with Luke.

Lando Calrissian™ reaches out
for a helping hand.

Leia and Luke make a daring exit.

The evil Emperor greets his minions while . . .

. . . the Rebel Alliance meets aboard *Home One*,
Admiral Ackbar's personal flagship.

A speeder bike explodes—and a stormtrooper is ejected.

Wicket the Ewok—a tiny warrior.

Who could have set such a primitive trap?

Chief Chirpa demanded the bidding of C-3PO.

"In time you will call me 'Master,'" the Emperor
tells Luke.

Will Luke turn Darth Vader away from the dark side
of the Force?

Stormtroopers take over!

Stronger and wiser than ever, Luke battles Vader.

An enemy AT-ST contains a welcome surprise—Chewbacca!

"Just for once let me look on you with my own eyes."

Luke reveals the truth to Leia.

with Chewbacca. Leia and Luke exchanged nervous glances, then smiled despite themselves.

Chewbacca and Han made their way down to the area below, silently positioning themselves behind two large trees near the pair of scout troopers. As one of the scouts picked up a black bag of supplies, Han stepped out from his hiding place and moved toward the scout's back. Everything seemed to be going fine until Han accidentally stepped on a dry twig. *Snap!*

The scout whirled and lashed out with his free arm, knocking Han off his feet. Han fired his blaster, sending a single laserbolt skyward before he fell back against the ground. The scout turned to his companion and shouted, "Go for help! Go!"

Luke and Leia saw the second scout run for his speeder bike. "Great!" Luke said sarcastically. "Come on." He and Leia jumped up from behind the fallen tree and ran down the hill.

Han rose fast, seized the scout who'd struck him, and threw him hard against the nearest tree. The other scout jumped onto his speeder bike and took off. Chewbacca stepped out from the trees, raised his Wookiee bowcaster, and squeezed off two shots after the scout. The first laserbolt whizzed past the speeder bike, but the second hit its mark and the speeder bike crashed into a tree; the scout went sailing over the bike's handgrip controls and hit the ground with bone-crunching impact.

Han was still fighting the first scout when Leia and Luke arrived near Chewbacca. Then Leia sighted another pair of scout troopers and shouted, "Over there! Two more of them!"

Luke followed Leia's gaze. The two scouts were already mounted on their speeder bikes — they looked back at Luke and Leia before racing off at high speed.

"I see them," Luke said, but Leia was already running for the remaining speeder bike, the one that belonged to the scout that was keeping Han occupied. "Wait, Leia!" Luke shouted. Running after her, he jumped onto the back of the bike just as Leia gripped and twisted the accelerator. Leia felt Luke's arms tighten around her waist as they launched forward into the forest.

Han turned in time to see Leia and Luke speeding off. "Hey, wait!" he called out. His white-armored opponent lunged for him. "Ahhh!" Han bellowed as he grabbed the scout's wrist and forearm and flipped him to the ground, finally knocking him out.

Luke and Leia hurtled after the two fleeing scouts. Leaning forward so Leia could hear him over the whine of the speeder's engine, Luke said, "Quick! Jam their comlink. Center switch!"

Leia pressed the switch, then accelerated. Branches

and leaves whipped past them as they followed the two scouts through the dense woodland. The scouts maneuvered over a fallen tree leaning against a cluster of other trees. Luke ducked as Leia successfully gained on the scouts by steering through the gap between the fallen tree and the ground.

"Move closer!" Luke said.

Leia gunned the engine. The two scouts veered recklessly through the woods, but Leia stayed with them. When one of the scouts fell behind, Luke saw an opportunity and said, "Get alongside that one!"

Leia accelerated again, then swung hard to the left until her directional vanes scraped against the scout's speeder bike. A cluster of trees forced Leia to break away from the scout, but while both speeders were still traveling at parallel trajectories, Luke leaped to the back of the scout's bike.

Landing behind the scout, Luke grabbed the scout's neck and twisted hard. The violent action flipped the scout right off the speeder and into a thick tree trunk. As the scout's body fell limp to the base of the tree, Luke reached for the bike's handgrips and quickly gained control.

Leia was slightly ahead of Luke, but he caught up with her. The remaining scout was straight in front of them. Luke shouted, "Get him!" But as they chased the scout around a wide group of trees, they drew the attention of two more bike-mounted scout troopers who were stationed in the forest.

The two scouts zoomed after Luke and Leia. One of the scouts fired twice, and a laserbolt glanced off the back of Luke's speeder. Luke looked back, then shouted to Leia, "Keep on that one!" He tilted his helmeted head toward the single bike in front of them. "I'll take these two!"

Luke stomped on his braking pedals and his speeder bike rapidly decelerated. Not anticipating his maneuver, Luke's two pursuers were startled as they flew by him on either side and suddenly found themselves in front of their prey. Luke launched forward, deployed his speeder bike's blaster cannon, and squeezed off a rapid burst of laserbolts at one of the scout troopers.

His aim was good. A shot connected, and the scout trooper's speeder bike went out of control and straight into a tree. The explosion was incredible. The other scout looked back to see the explosion, then faced forward and shifted into turbo drive, going even faster. Luke kept on his tail.

Far ahead of Luke, Leia was still chasing the single scout who'd evaded Han and Chewbacca. As the woods grew thicker up ahead, Leia decided to try a different tactic and aimed her bike skyward. Rising above the ground, she traveled fast under the forest canopy until she was almost directly above her quarry. Looking down, she saw the scout glance back behind him, trying to find her but failing.

Leia adjusted her bike's belly-mounted blaster cannon and fired. The scout's bike took a hit but kept on going. Leia descended from above and moved alongside him.

The scout reached to his right leg and drew a black compact blaster from his holster. Before Leia could react, he fired and scored a direct hit on her bike.

I've lost control! Leia dived off her bike just a split second before it slammed into a tree and exploded, spraying metal and plastoid everywhere. Her body tumbled to the ground.

Hearing the explosion, the scout glanced back with satisfaction to see the blast. But when he turned to face forward, he saw he was on a collision course for a giant, uprooted tree. He stomped on his brakes to no avail, then disappeared in a conflagration.

Lying on the ground where she'd landed, Leia heard the explosion. She lifted her dazed head once, then passed out.

Luke was unaware of Leia's condition and whereabouts as he chased the remaining scout through the trees. Luke moved in close, but the scout responded by slamming his bike into Luke's.

A fallen tree formed a bridge across their path. The scout zipped under the tree and Luke went over, then crashed his bike down on the scout's. The scout kept going. Both Luke and the scout looked ahead to see a wide trunk looming directly in Luke's path. Luke banked with all his might, leaning almost horizontally over the scout's bike to just barely make it past the trunk. He straightened out quickly, but his sudden maneuver caused his bike's steering vanes to lock onto the scout's. Then Luke saw another tree in his path.

Reacting instinctively, Luke dived off his bike and rolled to the ground. Freed from his weight, his bike came apart from the scout's, then lifted into the oncoming tree and exploded. Luke rose fast and saw the scout sweep out and away from the crash site and circle back through the forest.

He's coming back for me! Luke ignited his lightsaber just as the scout opened fire with his blaster cannon. Swinging his weapon, Luke deflected the fired laserbolts.

The scout kept shooting and aimed his bike straight for Luke. Luke batted away more laserbolts. When the scout's bike was almost on top of him, he stepped aside and swung at the bike's steering vanes, slicing them off. The scout's shattered bike hurtled forward, then began pitching and rolling as it slammed directly into a tree. In a fiery explosion, the last scout was gone.

Luke pulled off his helmet and tried to catch his

breath. He wondered about Leia, but thought, *If she were in any danger, I'm sure I would have sensed it.*

He was less certain about how far he was from where he'd left the Rebel strike team. Fortunately, he had a good enough sense of direction to know how to find his way back.

Luke deactivated his lightsaber and started running through the woods.

Slumped against the trunk of an immense tree, Han and Chewbacca were worried about Leia and Luke. The twelve SpecForces commandos were positioned around the area, watching for any sign of the princess or Luke. C-3PO stood beside R2-D2, whose extendable scanner antenna rotated back and forth above his domed head. Detecting movement nearby, R2-D2 beeped.

"Oh, General Solo," C-3PO said, "somebody's coming."

Han, Chewbacca, and the other soldiers raised their weapons and darted for cover. C-3PO and R2-D2 hid by a tree. Hearing approaching footsteps, C-3PO leaned out from behind the tree and said, "Oh!"

A forest-camouflaged form ran into the clearing. It was Luke.

"Luke!" Han said, stepping out from his hiding place. "Where's Leia?"

Panting hard from his run, Luke was suddenly concerned and alarmed. "What?" he asked. "She didn't come back?"

"I thought she was with you," Han replied.

"We got separated." Luke exchanged a silent, grim look with Han, then said, "Hey, we better go look for her."

Han nodded, then signaled to a Rebel officer. "Take the squad ahead. We'll meet at the shield generator at oh three hundred."

"Come on, Artoo," Luke said. "We'll need your scanners."

As Luke, Han, Chewbacca, and the droids moved off in one direction and the commandos proceeded in another, C-3PO said, "Don't worry, Master Luke. We know what to do." Then he glanced back at R2-D2 and added, "And you said it was pretty here. Ugh!"

CHAPTER 8

A small, fur-covered figure had been traveling through the woods, using his stone-tipped spear as a walking stick, when he'd heard the sound of speeder bikes traveling at high speed. A native of Endor's forest moon, he was aware of the presence of white-armored invaders on his world, but he had still been surprised when his large black eyes had sighted a bright flash of light in the distance: A speeder bike had crashed and exploded against a tree. That explosion had been followed by another, and then the sound of speeder bikes was gone.

The native didn't know the origin of the white-armored invaders, but he knew they weren't friendly. Because of what they'd been doing on his world — cutting down trees, erecting large metal structures, racing around on noisy machines — he neither liked nor welcomed them.

Now, adjusting his brown leather cowl, he listened and watched the forest. Except for the cries of some alarmed birds, he heard nothing and saw no movement around the area of the explosions. After waiting to make sure no other invaders were coming, he tightened his grip on his spear and moved quickly through the bushes and past the trees, making his way toward the crash sites. If the explosions had started any fires, he would put them out. If there were any survivors, he would deal with them, too.

The furry creature was an Ewok, and his name was Wicket.

Fortunately, the crashed speeder bikes had not left any flaming wreckage. Wicket found a lifeless white-armored form near the shattered remains of one bike, but the prone figure near the other crash site was different. For one thing, this particular invader wasn't wearing white armor, but was clad in garments that had been colored to blend in with the forest; also, watching the camouflage poncho's subtle rise and fall, Wicket could see the invader was breathing.

Wicket guessed the unconscious outsider had fallen or jumped from the speeder bike immediately before it crashed. Stepping closer, he saw she wore a helmet that revealed a human face. Wicket had encountered humans before, and the face reminded him of an adult woman whose family's star cruiser crash-landed on Endor. Then he remembered another woman, an evil shape-shifting witch, and shuddered at the memory.

Wicket assumed the human before him was a woman, but didn't assume she was friendly. Approaching her body cautiously, he extended his spear and prodded her side. When no reaction came, he prodded again.

Feeling the spear's jab, Princess Leia sat bolt upright and said, "Cut it out!"

Wicket jumped back but kept his spear held high.

Leia felt disoriented, but seeing the furry creature before her, it took all of her diplomatic skills to resist laughing. He was barely one meter tall, and despite his fierce behavior, he looked almost ridiculously adorable. Wondering how long she'd been unconscious, Leia stood up slowly and stretched. *No broken bones, thank goodness.*

The creature chittered at her.

"I'm not gonna hurt you," Leia said. She looked around at the charred remains of her speeder bike, then sighed and sat down on a fallen log. "Well, looks like I'm stuck here. Trouble is, I don't know where here is." She looked to the furry creature. "Maybe you can help me." She patted the log beside her. "Come on, sit down."

Wicket growled at her.

"I promise I won't hurt you," Leia continued gently. "Now come here." She patted the log again, and again the creature growled. "All right. You want something to eat?" She removed a ration bar from a pocket and held it out to him. She broke off a small piece and popped it into her own mouth, just to show him it wasn't poisonous.

Wicket cocked his head, looking at the bar, then took a cautious step forward onto the log. He chattered to her in his squeaky Ewok language.

"That's right," Leia said. "Come on. Hmmm?"

Sniffing the proffered food curiously, Wicket moved closer and took it from Leia's hand. Then he plopped himself down beside her and began nibbling at the bar. But when Leia reached up to remove her helmet, Wicket became startled. He jumped back and again raised his spear at her.

Leia held the helmet out to him and said, "Look, it's a hat. It's not gonna hurt you. Look." She showed him the helmet was empty. Reassured, he lowered his spear and took the helmet from her to examine it. Leia went on, "You're a jittery little thing, aren't you?"

Suddenly, Wicket turned away from Leia, dropping her helmet so he could grasp his spear with both paws. His ears perked up and he began to sniff the air. He looked around warily, and whispered an Ewokese warning to Leia.

"What is it?" Leia asked. Scanning the surrounding trees, she saw nothing.

Without warning, a laserbolt zinged out of the foliage and exploded on the log next to Leia. She and Wicket rolled backward off the log to hide behind it. Leia drew her blaster pistol and held it ready, peeking over the log as another laserbolt shot out from the forest and struck near her head.

Leia ducked down as Wicket threw himself into the small gap between the log and the ground. Leia thought, *Those shots were too precise to have been misses. Someone's trying to draw me out or scare me off.* She eased herself up again, risking another glance in the direction of the mysterious shooter, who remained completely concealed by trees.

"Freeze!" said a voice from just behind Leia, causing her to jump with surprise. She turned to see an Imperial scout trooper had snuck up on her. The scout had his blaster aimed at her head, and he reached out with his other hand to take her weapon.

"Come on, get up!" the scout ordered.

Leia rose and saw a second scout — the shooter — emerge from the dense foliage. Addressing the shooter, the scout beside her said, "Go get your ride and take her back to base."

"Yes, sir."

Still beneath the log, Wicket had seen enough to know that the woman was no friend of the white-armored invaders. Gripping his spear, the brave Ewok swung hard at the right leg of the scout beside Leia. *Whack!*

"What the —" exclaimed the scout, glancing down at Wicket.

Seizing the opportunity to take advantage of the distracted scout, Leia grabbed a fallen branch and swung at his head, knocking him out instantly. Then she dived for her blaster, came up with it fast, and aimed at the other scout, who'd just jumped onto his speeder bike. The bike took off, and Leia fired away at it.

The escaping scout's bike was hit, and he collided with the parked bike that belonged to his already-subdued companion. He was thrown head over heels through the air as both bikes exploded.

Wicket poked his fuzzy head up from behind the log and regarded Leia with new respect, muttering praise.

From her earlier run-in with scout troopers, Leia knew more could be close by. Holstering her blaster, she hurried over to her small ally and motioned for him to follow her away from the area.

"Come on," Leia said. "Let's get out of here."

But as they moved into the foliage, Wicket shrieked and tugged at Leia's arm. Figuring that her newfound friend knew his way around the forest better than she did, Leia decided to follow him. Both of them forgot about Leia's helmet, which remained on the ground where Wicket had dropped it.

*   *   *

On the Death Star, two Royal Guards stood sentry on either side of the turbolift in the Emperor's throne room. Neither guard so much as flinched when the turbolift door slid open and Darth Vader entered.

Vader crossed the bridge and ascended the stairway to the upper platform where the Emperor sat in his large chair, his back to the door. Gazing out the tall circular window, the Emperor chided, "I told you to remain on the command ship."

Vader said, "A small Rebel force has penetrated the shield and landed on Endor."

"Yes, I know," the Emperor replied in an almost bored tone as he slowly rotated his chair to face Vader.

Vader hesitated, wondering how much the Emperor really did know. Then he said, "My son is with them."

This did surprise the Emperor, but he tried not to show it.

"Are you sure?" he asked.

"I have *felt* him, my Master."

"Strange that I have not," the Emperor said testily. Leaning forward in his chair, he said, "I wonder if your feelings on this matter are clear, Lord Vader."

"They are clear, my Master."

"Then you must go to the Sanctuary Moon and wait for him."

Vader was skeptical. "He will come to me?"

"I have foreseen it," the Emperor said as he eased back into his chair. "His compassion for you will be his undoing. He will come to you, and then you will bring him before me."

"As you wish," Vader said, adding a deep bow. Then he turned and strode out of the throne room.

Luke reached down with his black-gloved right hand and picked up Leia's helmet from where it had been abandoned on the forest floor. *Oh, no*, he thought. *This doesn't look good.*

"Luke!" Han called out. "Luke!"

Carrying Leia's helmet, Luke ran to rejoin the search party. He found Han, Chewbacca, C-3PO, and R2-D2 beside the charred wreckage of a speeder bike in the grass.

"Oh, Master Luke," C-3PO said with dismay.

"There's two more wrecked speeders back there," Luke reported. "And I found this." He held out Leia's helmet, then tossed it to Han.

R2-D2 beeped.

C-3PO translated, "I'm afraid that Artoo's sensors can find no trace of Princess Leia."

Everyone looked to Han. Devastated, he said, "I hope she's all right."

Chewbacca sniffed at the air and growled. Then he walked off, pushing his way through the foliage.

"What, Chewie?" Han said.

Chewbacca barked but kept moving.

"*What*, Chewie?" Han repeated.

The group followed the Wookiee until he arrived at a break in the dense undergrowth. A tall wooden stake had been planted in the ground, and a dead animal hung from it.

Everyone moved up around Chewbacca. Looking at the carcass, Han said, "Hey, I don't get it."

Chewbacca eyed the carcass and let out a hungry groan.

"Nah," Han said. "It's just a dead animal, Chewie."

Unable to resist, Chewbacca reached for the carcass.

Sensing danger, Luke jumped forward and said, "Chewie, wa-wait! Don't!"

Too late. Chewbacca had already pulled the animal from the stake, triggering the trap. A strong branch sprang and lifted above them, rapidly hauling up the net that had been concealed under the grass and leaves beneath their feet. The net wrapped tightly around the entire group, forcing them together as it lifted them high above the clearing.

R2-D2 was lying practically sideways at the bottom of the net, and let out a wild series of beeps and whistles. Chewbacca howled his regret.

"Nice work," Han said, his face pressed up against the side of the net. "Great, Chewie! Great! Always thinking with your stomach."

"Will you take it easy," Luke said. His right arm poked through the net, but the rest of his body was twisted up against the others. "Let's just figure out a way to get out of this thing." He tried to free his arm, but was unsuccessful. "Han, can you reach my lightsaber?"

"Yeah, sure." Han stretched forward, reaching out to Luke.

Hoping to help, R2-D2 opened a panel on his cylindrical body, extended a compact circular saw, and activated its rotating blade. Exhibiting a skill most often attributed to surgeons using trephines, the astromech began rapidly cutting through the net.

"Artoo," C-3PO said, "I'm not sure that's such a good idea. It's a very long dro-o-op!" C-3PO's last word was punctuated by the net tearing open, instantly releasing all the figures to tumble to the clearing below.

That hurt, Luke thought, pushing himself to sit up on the ground. He looked around. Han and Chewbacca appeared to be a bit stunned but were otherwise fine, and R2-D2 had somehow landed on his feet. *Where's Threepio?* Before he could sight the golden droid, he saw movement within some nearby ferns and bushes. Then short, fur-covered creatures emerged, pushing their way through the foliage to surround the fallen group.

The creatures were armed with primitive weapons: stone-tipped spears and knives, heavy wooden clubs, bows and arrows. They appeared to be hunters or warriors. Most had dark pelts, but one had light and dark gray-striped fur; he was further distinguished by an ornate headdress that had been made from the skull of a large animal, and a necklace of long, sharp teeth.

Two of the hunters moved up on either side of R2-D2 and brushed their paws against his exterior. R2-D2 beeped nervously.

Thinking the creatures were harmless, Han grinned at them. Evidently, this was an error; the hunter wearing the skull headdress — apparently the leader — stepped forward and jabbed the tip of his long spear at the air in front of Han's face.

"Wait . . ." Han said. "Hey!" He raised his hand and swatted at the spear. "Point that thing someplace else."

Han's antagonist turned to one of his furry companions and they had a quick, chittering discussion. A moment later, the stripe-furred creature angled his spear back at Han.

"Hey!" Han said again angrily, grabbing at the spear with one hand as he drew his blaster with the other.

"Han, don't," Luke cautioned. "It'll be all right." Luke sensed the creatures were merely trying to protect their territory and he didn't want to harm them. As a gesture of good faith, he removed his lightsaber from its belt clip and handed it over to one of the hunters.

Han's blaster was taken from him. Chewbacca was not so ready to relinquish his own weapon and growled in protest.

Luke said, "Chewie, give 'em your crossbow." The Wookiee growled again but complied.

"Oh, my head," C-3PO said as he sat up from a nearby bed of ferns. Then he saw all the weapon-wielding creatures and added, "Oh, my goodness!"

At the sight of the golden droid, the hunters gasped. Then they muttered to each other and lowered their weapons. Unexpectedly, they began to chant and bow down before C-3PO.

Chewbacca let out a puzzled bark. Han and Luke regarded the bowing creatures with wonder.

C-3PO turned his head from side to side, listening to the natives' language. Then he said, "Treetoe doggra. Ee soyoto ambuna nocka."

A few of the creatures responded in their own language. The others continued to bow and chant.

Looking to C-3PO, Luke asked, "Do you understand anything they're saying?"

"Oh, yes, Master Luke! Remember that I am fluent in over six million forms of communica —"

"What are you telling them?" Han interrupted.

"Hello, I think . . ." C-3PO said. "I could be mistaken. These creatures seem to call themselves 'Ewoks.' They're using a very primitive dialect. But I do believe they think I am some sort of god."

Chewbacca and R2-D2 found this extremely amusing. Han and Luke exchanged glances, then Han said sarcastically, "Well, why don't you use your divine influence and get us out of this?"

"I beg your pardon, General Solo," C-3PO said, "but that just wouldn't be proper."

Getting angry again, Han asked, "Proper?!"

"It's against my programming to impersonate a deity," C-3PO explained.

Moving threateningly toward the protocol droid, Han said, "Why, you . . ."

Several spears were suddenly thrust close to Han as the Ewoks moved to protect their newfound god. Han held up his hands placatingly and said, "My mistake. He's an old friend of mine."

Unfortunately, the Ewoks didn't think much of C-3PO's friends.

CHAPTER 9

A procession wound through the ever-darkening forest. Their prisoners — Han, Luke, Chewbacca, and R2-D2 — had been tied to long poles, each of which was dutifully carried on the shoulders of several Ewoks. Behind the bound captives, the remaining diminutive forest warriors carried a makeshift litter, on which C-3PO was seated like a king upon a throne made of sturdy branches and vines.

The procession moved along a shaky, narrow, wooden walkway that traveled high up to the giant trees. Soon, they reached the end of the walkway, which dropped off into nothingness. Across the abyss, a village of huts — made out of mud and sticks — and more rickety walkways wrapped around the trees. The lead Ewok took hold of a long vine and swung across to the village square. A rope bridge was extended, allowing the other Ewoks to carry C-3PO and the prisoners on to the village.

The procession wound its way into the village square. The Ewoks' tribal leader was the gray-furred Chief Chirpa, and he stepped out to greet the returning hunters. At the sight of the newcomers, mother Ewoks gathered up their babies and scurried into their huts.

The Ewoks carried C-3PO up to the largest hut and placed his wooden throne so he had a wide view of the square. Still bound to the poles, Luke, Chewbacca, and R2-D2 were propped up against a tree while Han was lifted onto a spit. Han said, "I have a really bad feeling about this."

Chewbacca growled his concern.

All activity stopped as a tan-striped Ewok came out of the big hut. He was Logray, the tribal shaman and medicine man, and he wore the half skull of a great forest bird on his head. While Chief Chirpa examined Luke's lightsaber with great curiosity, Logray surveyed the captives, then went to stand beside C-3PO. Logray addressed the assembly and gestured at the prisoners.

"What did he say?" Han asked.

"I'm rather embarrassed, General Solo," C-3PO said, "but it appears you are to be the main course at a banquet in my honor."

As one group of Ewoks began beating on drums, another started placing firewood under Han's suspended body. Understandably, Han looked increasingly uncomfortable. It was at this moment that Leia and Wicket emerged from the large hut. Leia wore an animal-skin dress that the Ewoks had made for her, and her long hair was down. Seeing her friends in their present state, she was temporarily speechless.

Luke saw her first and was surprised by her appearance. "Leia?"

Han twisted his neck to follow Luke's gaze. "Leia!"

Leia moved toward them, but the Ewok warriors raised their spears and blocked her path. "Oh!" Leia said.

"Your Royal Highness," C-3PO said from his throne, happy to be reunited with the princess.

Leia looked at the Ewoks and sighed. Gesturing to the captives, she said, "But these are my friends. Threepio, tell them they must be set free."

C-3PO remained seated as he quickly conversed with Chirpa and Logray. The two Ewoks listened, then shook their heads negatively. Logray gestured toward the prisoners and barked some orders. Hearing Logray's command, more Ewoks joined in to pile wood under Han.

"Somehow," Han said, "I got the feeling that didn't help us very much."

Luke suddenly realized he might be able to use the Ewoks' superstitious nature against them. He said, "Threepio, tell them if they don't do as you wish, you'll become angry and use your magic."

Baffled, C-3PO protested, "But Master Luke, what magic? I couldn't possibly —"

"Just tell them," Luke said.

All the Ewoks stopped what they were doing and turned to C-3PO as he said, "Horomee ana fu, toron togosh! Toron Togosh! Terro way. Qee t'woos twotoe ai. U wee di dozja. Boom!"

Many Ewoks jumped at the last word, but Logray stepped forward and challenged C-3PO, calling his bluff. The drumming resumed.

Luke closed his eyes and concentrated.

"You see, Master Luke," C-3PO said. "They didn't believe me. Just as I said they wouldn't."

Han saw some Ewoks carrying small torches toward him. He said, "Hey, wait —!" then stopped talking so he could puff his cheeks and start blowing at the flames in a desperate effort to put them out.

The golden droid didn't immediately realize Luke was using the Force to levitate his throne. Rising higher over the deck, C-3PO's arms started waving and he cried, "What-wha-what's happening! Oh, dear! Oh!"

The Ewoks fell back in terror from the floating throne. Then C-3PO began to spin as though he were on a revolving stool. In a state of total panic, he shouted, "Put me down! He-e-elp. Somebody help! Master Luke! Artoo! Somebody, somebody, help! Master Luke, Artoo, Artoo, quickly! Do something, some-body! Oh! Ohhh!"

Logray yelled orders to the cowering Ewoks. They rushed up and released the bound prisoners. One Ewok used a small stone ax to cut the restraints that secured R2-D2, and the astromech pitched forward and crashed to the wooden deck. The Ewoks helped him up, but R2-D2 was fighting mad. He beeped angrily at Teebo, the nearest Ewok, the same gray-striped leader of the group who'd captured the droid and his friends. R2-D2 opened a panel and zapped Teebo with an electrical charge. Teebo hollered and jumped away. R2-D2 gave him another zap.

Freed from his bonds, Luke continued to use the Force to slowly return C-3PO's throne to the deck. As the droid descended and gently landed, he said, "Oh, oh, oh, oh! Thank goodness."

Luke joined Leia, Chewbacca, and a very relieved Han beside Chief Chirpa's hut. Luke looked to the golden droid and said, "Thanks, Threepio."

Still shaken, C-3PO admitted, "I . . . never knew I had it in me."

Night fell on the forest moon, and the entire Ewok tribe tried to squeeze into Chief Chirpa's hut to listen to C-3PO's fireside story. The hut had a spacious in-terior, but some of the Ewoks had to stand outside and lean in through the windows in order to hear.

Illuminated by the glowing fire at the center of the hut, C-3PO was in the midst of a long, animated tale. Chief Chirpa sat on his small wooden throne next to Logray and the village elders. Leia and Han sat together near Chewbacca and R2-D2. Luke stood near an open doorway at the back of the room. As the droid spoke, Wicket came up beside Han and snuggled against his leg.

Although C-3PO had always maintained that he wasn't much of a storyteller, he was very entertaining as he presented a short history of the Galactic Civil War. He pointed several times to the Rebels in the room, and made pantomime movements accompanied by his own audio mimickry of starship engines and explosions. After he described Obi-Wan Kenobi's duel with Darth Vader and imitated the sounds of lightsabers clashing, R2-D2 began beeping excitedly.

"Yes, Artoo," C-3PO said. "I was just coming to that." He resumed his story, and the Ewoks were completely captivated by his account of the Battle of Hoth, Han Solo's ordeal on Cloud City, and their recent escape from Jabba's palace.

When C-3PO was done, Chief Chirpa, Logray, and the elders conferred, then nodded in agreement. Chirpa stood and made a brief pronouncement.

Watching the Ewoks, Han leaned closer to Leia and asked, "What's going on?"

"I don't know," Leia replied.

The Ewok elders talked with C-3PO, who then turned to Leia and Han and exclaimed, "Wonderful! We are now a part of the tribe."

"Just what I always wanted," Han said as more Ewoks swarmed over him with hugs. Other Ewoks began banging rhythmically on their drums, and Chief Chirpa's hut was filled with happy, screeching cheers.

Luke's lightsaber had been returned to him, and as he watched his friends celebrate, he was suddenly overcome by a feeling of dread. *It seems so safe here, but it won't last . . . not so long as the Emperor reigns.* He turned for the doorway and stepped out into the night. He didn't notice that Leia had seen his exit.

Chewbacca was being mobbed by young Ewoks, who were endlessly amazed by the Wookiee's height. The Wookiee barked to Han.

Han said, "Well, short help is better than no help at all, Chewie." Then Han found himself receiving another embrace from Wicket. Han grinned and said, "Thank you."

Han broke away from Wicket and moved up behind C-3PO, who was engaged in conversation with Chief Chirpa. Turning to Han, C-3PO translated, "He says the scouts are going to show us the quickest way to the shield generator."

"Good," Han said. "How far is it?" C-3PO looked

at Han blankly, so Han gestured to Chirpa and said, "*Ask* him."

C-3PO turned back to Chirpa and said, "Grau neeka —"

The golden droid stopped talking because Han was tapping his shoulder. He turned back to Han, who added, "We need some fresh supplies, too."

Returning his attention to Chirpa, C-3PO rephrased his question: "Chee oto pah —"

But Han tapped his shoulder again.

"And try to get our weapons back."

C-3PO turned back again to Chirpa, this time beginning, "Umma freeda —"

C-3PO felt Han grip his upper arm, forcing him to turn around again. Han said impatiently, "And hurry up, will ya? I haven't got all day."

Han walked off. C-3PO's head jerked back and forth, not knowing which way to turn. If he didn't know better, he would have sworn Han Solo was trying to confuse him.

Leia followed Luke outside. He was leaning against a rail on the torch-illuminated wooden walkway that extended from Chirpa's hut. Leia stepped up beside him and said, "Luke, what's wrong?"

Luke turned and looked at Leia for a long moment. "Leia . . . do you remember your mother? Your real mother?"

"Just a little bit," Leia said. "She died when I was very young."

"What do you remember?"

"Just . . . images, really. Feelings."

"Tell me."

Leia was surprised by Luke's curiosity, but responded, "She was very beautiful. Kind but . . . sad. Why are you asking me this?"

"I have no memory of my mother," Luke said sadly. "I never knew her."

"Luke, tell me. What's troubling you?"

Luke hesitated, then said, "Vader is here . . . now, on this moon."

"How do you know?" Leia asked with alarm.

"I felt his presence," Luke answered, lowering his gaze to stare at a plank on the walkway. "He's come for me. He can feel when I'm near. That's why I have to go." He looked at Leia and continued, "As long as I stay, I'm endangering the group and our mission here. I have to face him."

"Why?" For a moment, she wondered if Luke was seeking revenge after his last duel with Vader. She was hardly prepared for what he said next.

"He's my father."

"Your father?" Leia gasped, her face contorting in astonishment. The thought of Luke being related to Vader was horrific.

"There's more," Luke said. "It won't be easy for you to hear it, but you must. If I don't make it back, you're the only hope for the Alliance."

Disturbed by Luke's words, Leia moved slightly away from him. "Luke, don't talk that way. You have a power I . . . I don't understand and could never have."

"You're wrong, Leia. You have that power, too. In time you'll learn to use it as I have." Again, he looked away from her. He continued, "The Force is strong in my family. My father has it . . . I have it . . ." Then he looked to Leia as he added, ". . . and my sister has it."

Leia stared into Luke's eyes. What she saw there frightened her, but she didn't draw away. And she began to understand.

"Yes," Luke said. "It's you, Leia."

"I know. Somehow . . . I've always known."

"Then you know why I have to face him."

"No! Luke, run away, far away. If he can feel your presence, then leave this place. I wish I could go with you."

"No, you don't," Luke said. "You've always been strong."

"But why must you confront him?"

"Because . . . there is good in him. I've felt it. He won't turn me over to the Emperor. I can save him. I can turn him back to the good side. I have to try."

Leia was overwhelmed by conflicting emotions. Part of her wanted to believe Luke could save their father, and that their father was truly worth saving. Yet she also knew that Vader was responsible for countless atrocities. He'd even supervised her torture on the first Death Star, and cut off Luke's hand, and yet . . . *And yet he's our father. And Luke believes there's good in him.*

Luke and Leia held each other close. He kissed her cheek, then slowly let her go and moved off along the walkway. Han stepped out of the hut just in time to see Luke vanish into the darkness.

Han walked up toward Leia, then realized she was trembling. He stopped short and said, "Hey, what's goin' on?"

"Nothing," Leia replied. "I — just want to be alone for a little while."

"Nothing?" Han said, not buying it. "Come on, tell me. What's goin' on?"

Leia looked at him, struggling to control herself. "I . . . I can't tell you."

"Could you tell Luke?" Han fumed. "Is that who you could tell?"

"I — " Leia choked on her words.

Exasperated, Han said, "Ahhh . . ." He turned, storming off toward the hut. Then he stopped, suddenly realizing things were not what he'd thought they were. He turned to walk slowly back to Leia. He kept a short distance from her, and said, "I'm sorry."

Leia looked to Han and said, "Hold me."

And he did.

High in the pre-dawn sky of Endor's forest moon, the unfinished Death Star was clearly visible against the fading stars. Darth Vader's shuttle left the massive satellite and traveled down to the Imperial outpost that had been constructed on the moon. The outpost's largest structure was an energy shield generator: rising nearly 150 meters into the sky, it was a four-sided pyramid-shaped tower that supported a wide focus dish; the dish's central emitter antenna was directed to project a powerful deflector shield around the Death Star.

Near the shield generator, an elevated landing platform rested on two columnar turbolift housings and rose above an area that had been cleared of trees. As Vader's shuttle touched down on the floodlight-illuminated platform, a four-legged All Terrain Armored Transport walker lurched toward a gantry that extended below the platform and between the support columns.

Vader disembarked, proceeding to the platform's turbolift. Two stormtroopers accompanied him on his descent to the gantry level, where he emerged from the lift to find the AT-AT had docked with the platform. The AT-AT's hatch slid up to reveal an Imperial commander, three stormtroopers — and Luke Skywalker.

Luke's wrists were secured by binders. He gazed at Vader with complete calm.

The gray-uniformed commander stepped toward Vader and said, "This is a Rebel that surrendered to us. Although he denies it, I believe there may be more of them, and I request permission to conduct a further search of the area. He was armed only with this."

The commander handed Luke's lightsaber over to Vader. Vader said, "Good work, Commander. Leave us. Conduct your search and bring his companions to me."

"Yes, my lord." The commander signaled to the three stormtroopers, and he returned with them to the AT-AT.

Vader and Luke walked slowly toward the turbolift. Vader said, "The Emperor has been expecting you."

"I know, father."

Vader glanced at Luke and said, "So you have accepted the truth."

"I've accepted the truth that you were once Anakin Skywalker, my father."

Vader stopped to face Luke and said menacingly, "That name no longer has any meaning for me."

"It is the name of your true self," Luke replied. "You've only forgotten. I know there is good in you. The Emperor hasn't driven it from you fully." Looking away from Vader, Luke rested his arms on the gantry's railing and gazed at the surrounding forest. "That was why you couldn't destroy me," he continued. "That's why you won't bring me to your Emperor now."

Vader seemed to ponder Luke's words, then said, "I see you have constructed a new lightsaber." He ignited the brilliant green blade of Luke's weapon, and Luke — still facing away — stiffened as he heard its deadly hum.

Vader examined the lightsaber, admiring its craftsmanship. "Your skills are complete," he said. Turning his back to look away from Luke, he added, "Indeed, you are powerful, as the Emperor has foreseen."

Taking a cautious step forward, Luke pleaded. "Come with me."

"Obi-Wan once thought as you do," said the black-armored Sith Lord. He turned to face Luke. "You don't know the power of the dark side. I must obey my Master."

Luke shook his head. "I will not turn," he said boldly, "and you'll be forced to kill me."

Less certain of the future, Vader said, "If that is your destiny —"

"Search your feelings, father," Luke interrupted. "You can't do this. I feel the conflict within you. Let go of your hate."

If only I could, Vader thought. *If only I could.*

He said, "It is too late for me, son." Then he signaled to the two stormtroopers who'd been waiting by the turbolift. The troopers stepped up behind Luke as Vader said, "The Emperor will show you the true nature of the Force. He is your Master now."

Vader and Luke stared at each other, until Luke broke the silence and said, "Then my father is truly dead."

The younger Skywalker walked directly into the turbolift, with the two stormtroopers sticking close beside him. Inside the lift, he turned to face his father, who remained on the gantry, looking at him. Then the lift door slid shut, leaving Vader alone on the gantry.

Vader stepped to the railing and tried to collect his thoughts. *I must obey my Master. I must deliver Luke to him. But if Luke can kill the Emperor, perhaps . . . perhaps then I will be free.*

Vader saw the sun was beginning to rise. He turned away from the railing and returned to the turbolift.

CHAPTER 10

At the predesignated time of 0300, Princess Leia, Han Solo, Chewbacca, the droids, and their two Ewok guides — Wicket and a scout named Paploo — met up with Major Derlin and the other eleven Spec-Forces Rebel commandos. Shortly after dawn, the group arrived at a ridge that overlooked the Imperial shield generator and landing platform. On the landing platform, an Imperial *Lambda*-class shuttle lifted off, extended its lower wings, and flew skyward, on course for the Death Star.

Leia had changed back into her Rebel uniform and camouflage poncho. Surveying the Imperial outpost, she said, "The main entrance to the control bunker's on the far side of that landing platform. This isn't going to be easy."

"Hey, don't worry," Han said. "Chewie and me got into a lot of places more heavily guarded than this."

Wicket and Paploo chattered to each other, then spoke to C-3PO. Leia turned to the golden droid and asked, "What's he saying?"

C-3PO translated, "He says there's a secret entrance on the other side of the ridge."

Paploo knew a shortcut. The Rebels followed him.

In the Sullust system, the Rebel fleet prepared for their flight to the Death Star. Lando Calrissian was in the cockpit of the *Millennium Falcon*. His copilot was the Sullustan Nien Nunb. Behind them, two Rebel soldiers checked and adjusted the *Falcon*'s navigational and shield controls.

Lando guided the *Falcon* past the larger battle cruisers. He was followed by a group of single-pilot starfighters that included X-wings, A-wings, B-wings, and Y-wings.

"Admiral, we're in position," Lando reported into his comlink. "All fighters accounted for."

"Proceed with the countdown," Admiral Ackbar's voice answered from the comm. "All groups assume attack coordinates."

Nien Nunb checked his controls and muttered something in his native tongue. He sounded nervous.

"Don't worry," Lando said, "my friend's down there. He'll have that shield down on time." As Nien Nunb flipped some switches, Lando continued to himself, "Or this'll be the shortest offensive of all time."

From the Mon Cal cruiser, Admiral Ackbar said, "All craft, prepare to jump into hyperspace on my mark."

"All right," Lando replied. "Stand by." At Ackbar's signal, he pulled a lever and the stars suddenly appeared to streak past the cockpit window as the *Falcon* roared into hyperspace. The *Falcon* was quickly followed by the single-pilot starfighters. Then Ackbar's cruiser and the other larger vessels vanished in the same direction, until the entire Rebel armada was en route to the Endor system at faster-than-light speed.

On Endor, Paploo arrived beside some bushes along a ridge, then turned and whistled to Wicket and the Rebels. Leia, Han, and the others spread through the thick undergrowth along the ridge, looking down from their position to see the control bunker that led into the base of the energy shield generator. Outside the bunker entrance was a clearing where four Imperial scout troopers stood, with their speeder bikes parked nearby.

Chewbacca growled an observation, and Paploo chattered in Ewokese to Han.

Han said, "Back door, huh? Good idea."

Wicket and Paploo asked C-3PO to explain what the Rebels hoped to accomplish. When C-3PO finished, the two Ewoks had a quick exchange, then Paploo jumped up and scampered into the bushes.

Leia moved close beside Han. Looking at the Imperial scouts, Han observed, "It's only a few guards. This shouldn't be too much trouble."

Remembering Han's last encounter with a group of scout troopers, Leia said, "Well, it only takes one to sound the alarm."

Ever confident, Han grinned and said, "Then we'll do it real quiet-like."

C-3PO asked Wicket where Paploo had gone. Wicket told him. Startled, C-3PO exclaimed, "Oh! Oh, my. Uh, Princess Leia!"

Leia turned around and clamped her hand over C-3PO's vocabulator. When he settled down, she removed her hand. C-3PO lowered his voice and said, "I'm afraid our furry companion has gone and done something rather rash."

Chewbaca barked. Leia, Han, and the others watched in distress as Paploo emerged from the bushes below them. He was only a short distance away from the scout troopers.

"Oh, no," Leia said.

Han sighed. "There goes our surprise attack."

Paploo silently pulled his furry body up onto one of the parked speeder bikes, then began flipping switches at random. Suddenly the bike's engine fired up with a tremendous roar.

"Look!" shouted one of the scout troopers. "Over there! Stop him!" The scouts raced toward Paploo just as his speeder bike launched into the forest at incredible speed. The little Ewok clung tight to the handgrip controls and shrieked.

Three of the Imperial scouts jumped onto the remaining speeder bikes and sped away to pursue the bike thief. All the fourth scout could do was stand at his post and watch them go.

Up on the ridge, Leia, Han, and Chewbacca exchanged delighted looks. Han said, "Not bad for a little furball. There's only one left." Turning to C-3PO, he added, "You stay here. We'll take care of this."

As Han and Chewbacca moved off toward the bunker, C-3PO stepped over beside Wicket and R2-D2. The golden droid declared, "I have decided that we shall stay here."

R2-D2 beeped his concern for Paploo, but the little Ewok was actually enjoying his swift ride through the forest. At the moment, Paploo's only physical contact with the speeder bike was his paws wrapped around the controls; the rest of his body was airborne, suspended over the bike's saddle. He felt like he was flying.

Maintaining his grip on the controls, Paploo maneuvered his body so he was partially perched on the saddle. The three Imperial scouts came up fast behind him. When one of the scouts had the Ewok in his sights, he fired his bike's blaster cannon. The laserbolt struck the back of Paploo's bike. Paploo was unharmed, but his bike went into a dizzying roll.

The Ewok somehow reoriented his spinning bike, then steered into a sharp curve around a tree. Another laserbolt whizzed past him, and he decided it was time to get off.

He sighted a long vine dangling in his path. He released his bike's controls, grabbed a dangling vine, and swung up high into the trees. A moment later, the three scouts tore under him in pursuit of his still-flying, rider-less bike.

Back at the bunker, Han snuck up behind the remaining Imperial scout. Han tapped him on the shoulder, then turned and ran around the bunker, letting the scout chase him. When the scout came around the bunker's corner, he was confronted by the waiting and armed Rebel strike team. Demonstrating some wisdom, the scout surrendered immediately.

Han pressed a control switch in the bunker's doorway and the door slid open. With their weapons drawn, Han, Leia, Chewbacca, and four Rebel commandos entered the bunker's dark interior. The door slid closed behind them.

On the Death Star, in the tower high above the space station's north pole, Darth Vader and Luke — his wrists still secured by binders — arrived at the

Emperor's throne room. As before, two Royal Guards stood silently on either side of the turbolift door. Exiting the turbolift, Vader and Luke crossed the bridge over the elevator shaft, then ascended the stairway to stand before the Emperor.

"Welcome, young Skywalker," the Emperor said from his throne. "I have been expecting you."

Luke had never seen the Emperor before. The Emperor's hooded visage was disfigured: flesh sagged from his bulging forehead and around his piercing yellow eyes — even his voice sounded ravaged by the evil that flowed through his veins. Luke gazed at him defiantly and thought, *He looks like a corpse.*

The Emperor smiled, displaying rotten teeth as he glanced at the binders on Luke's wrists. He said, "You no longer need those," then made a slight gesture with his finger. The binders fell away and clattered noisily against the floor.

Luke looked down at his hands, then back at the Emperor. He thought, *It's as if he's inviting me to try and kill him with my bare hands. And he looks so weak.* But Luke had learned from Ben and Yoda that looks could be deceiving, so he remained standing where he was, at Vader's side.

The Emperor glanced at his red acolytes and commanded, "Guards, leave us." The two red-armored sentries turned and disappeared behind the turbolift.

Then the Emperor returned his gaze to Luke and said, "I'm looking forward to completing your training. In time you will call *me* Master."

"You're gravely mistaken," Luke replied. "You won't convert me as you did my father."

"Oh, no, my young Jedi," said the Emperor, rising from his throne threateningly to step closer to Luke. "You will find that it is *you* who are mistaken . . . about a great many things."

Vader said, "His lightsaber," and presented Luke's weapon to the Emperor.

Taking the lightsaber, the Emperor said, "Ah, yes, a Jedi's weapon. Much like your father's. By now you must know your father can never be turned from the dark side. So will it be with you."

"You're wrong," Luke said. "Soon I'll be dead . . . and you with me."

The Emperor laughed. "Perhaps you refer to the imminent attack of your Rebel fleet."

Luke looked up sharply. *He knows.*

"Yes," hissed the Emperor, "I assure you we are quite safe from your friends here." He turned to walk back to his throne.

"Your overconfidence is your weakness," Luke stated.

The Emperor stopped and glanced back at Luke. With a sneer, he replied, "Your faith in your friends is yours."

He's wrong, Luke hoped. *He's so wrong.*

Vader said, "It is pointless to resist, my son."

The Emperor eased back into his throne and faced Luke. "Everything that has transpired has done so according to *my* design," he said. "Your friends up there on the Sanctuary Moon are walking into a trap. As is your Rebel fleet!"

Oh, no, Luke thought. *No!*

The Emperor continued, "It was *I* who allowed the Alliance to know the location of the shield generator. It is quite safe from your pitiful little band. An entire legion of my best troops awaits them."

Luke looked from the Emperor to Vader, then to his lightsaber, which remained in the Emperor's clutches.

The Emperor leaned forward in his throne. In a tone that reeked of mock sympathy, he said, "Oh . . . I'm afraid the deflector shield will be quite operational when your friends arrive."

On Endor, inside the Imperial bunker, Han, Leia, Chewbacca, and the Rebel strike team stormed through a door and entered the main control room. There they found an Imperial officer standing beside three black-uniformed generator controllers; the startled men turned away from their computer consoles to see the armed Rebels.

"All right!" Han shouted at the controllers. "Up! Move! Come on! Quickly! Quickly! Chewie!"

Chewbacca growled and leveled his bowcaster at the controllers. Behind him, an open doorway offered a view of the turbine generator chamber that powered the energy shield that was projected at the Death Star. A blaster-wielding Imperial officer came running in from the generator chamber, but an alert Rebel commando knocked him out.

As the controllers were herded away from their consoles, Leia glanced at a viewscreen that displayed a two-dimensional graphic of the shield-protected Death Star. Checking a chronometer, she said, "Han! Hurry! The fleet will be here any moment."

Han turned to one of the Rebel commandos and said, "Charges! Come on, come on!" The commando tossed a bag of proton grenades to Han.

Outside the bunker, C-3PO, R2-D2, and Wicket were still watching from the bushes when they saw several stormtroopers and controllers suddenly emerge from the surrounding forest. The Imperial soldiers rushed to the bunker's doorway and entered.

Realizing that their allies were probably unaware of the incoming Imperial troops, C-3PO cried, "Oh, my! They'll be captured!"

Wicket chattered urgently in Ewokese, then darted away from the droids and into the forest.

"Wa-ait!" C-3PO wailed. "Wait, come back!" He clapped a hand down on top of R2-D2's dome and said, "Artoo, stay with me."

Back inside the main control room, Han was about to plant an explosive charge when an Imperial officer appeared in the doorway that overlooked the turbine generator and said, "Freeze!"

Han spun fast and threw a bag of explosives at the officer. The officer cried out as the bag hit him in the chest and carried him over the railing behind him. Before Han could make another move, an overwhelming number of stormtroopers flooded into the control room.

Han, Leia, and the others had no choice but to relinquish their weapons. Chewbacca howled in anger.

A black-uniformed Imperial commander walked up to Han and said, "You Rebel scum."

The *Millennium Falcon* dropped out of hyperspace and blasted into the Endor system. In the *Falcon*'s cockpit, Lando and Nien Nunb looked through their window to see Endor's forest moon and the unfinished Death Star, which appeared to grow larger with each passing second of their approach. Lando glanced at his sensor scopes and watched dozens of blips appear as the rest of the Imperial fleet emerged from hyperspace behind him.

Lando's comm unit designation for the mission was Gold Leader. He said into his comlink, "All wings report in."

"Red Leader standing by," Wedge Antilles answered from his X-wing starfighter.

"Gray Leader standing by," came the reply from a Y-wing.

"Green Leader standing by," said the commander of the A-wing starfighters.

Wedge said, "Lock S-foils in attack positions." Wedge's squadron included S-foil-equipped X-wings and B-wings; in response to his command, the X-wing pilots unlocked their wing-connecting assemblies to spread their double-layered wings, and the B-wings' cannon-tipped airfoils extended from their primary wings.

All the Rebel ships headed straight for the Death Star. On the Mon Cal cruiser, Admiral Ackbar watched the starfighters massing outside his viewport and said, "May the Force be with us."

In the *Falcon*'s cockpit, Nien Nunb tried to get a reading on the Death Star's energy shield but found nothing on his scopes. He pointed to the control panel and said, "Ah-teh-yairee u-hareh mu-ah-hareh."

Fortunately, Lando understood his Sullustan copilot and replied, "We've got to be able to get *some* kind of a reading on that shield, up or down."

Nien Nunb could imagine only one possibilty: The Death Star was using long-range sensor jammers to deceive the Rebel fleet. "Mu-ah-hareh mu-kay, huh?" he asked.

Lando said, "Well, how could they be jamming us if they don't know . . . we're coming." And then Lando realized the truth: *They know.* Somehow the Empire had anticipated the Rebel assault.

"Break off the attack!" Lando yelled into his comlink. "The shield is still up."

"I get no reading," Wedge answered over the comm. "Are you sure?"

"Pull up!" Lando ordered. "All craft pull up!" The *Falcon* and the fighters of Red Squad veered off desperately to avoid the invisible energy shield.

Inside Admiral Ackbar's cruiser, alarms sounded. "Take evasive action!" Ackbar commanded his crew. Turning to a comlink, he said, "Green Group, stick close to holding sector MV-Seven."

A Mon Calamari controller called out, "Admiral, we have enemy ships in sector forty-seven."

Ackbar swiveled in his seat to face the controller and said, "It's a trap."

Sure enough, the *Falcon* and the other ships had veered straight for an armada of Imperial Star Destroyers. At a glance, Lando guessed there were about twenty. He recognized the largest vessel — a *Super*-class Star Destroyer — as the same ship that had nearly captured the *Falcon* after he'd helped rescue Luke from Cloud City.

Then Lando saw the TIE fighters.

"Fighters coming in," he said into his comlink. It

was an understatement. Hundreds of TIE fighters were streaking away from the Star Destroyers and racing for the Rebel fleet. Most of the Imperial fighters were Interceptors, identifiable by their bent and elongated dagger-shaped solar collector panels. The Interceptors were the latest in Twin Ion Engine design, and were far more lethal than standard TIE fighters. In an instant, dozens of fierce dogfights ensued around the giant Mon Cal cruisers.

Lando adjusted the *Falcon's* targeting computer so he could fire the turbolaser cannons from the cockpit. The number of speeding TIE fighters and all the crisscrossing streaks of laserfire were so overwhelming that it was almost impossible to see the stars beyond the battle zone. Nien Nunb steered after a pair of TIE fighters and Lando fired the *Falcon's* cannons.

"There's too many of them!" a Rebel pilot shouted from his starfighter's cockpit. A moment later, the pilot's ship was struck by enemy fire and was gone.

Flying through the battle, Lando ordered, "Accelerate to attack speed! Draw their fire away from the cruisers."

"Copy, Gold Leader," Wedge answered, and instructed his X-wing squad to follow his lead. The starfighters angled off from the larger Rebel ships.

High atop the Death Star, the space battle was visible through the tall circular window behind the Emperor's throne. From his seat, the Emperor faced Luke and said, "Come, boy. See for yourself."

Luke moved toward the window. In the distance, Rebel and Imperial starfighters appeared as swirling pinpoints of light. Laserfire streaked between the fighters. There were many explosions.

The Emperor said, "From here you will witness the final destruction of the Alliance and the end of your insignificant Rebellion."

Luke's lightsaber rested on the right arm of the Emperor's throne. The Emperor extended his bony fingers to the lightsaber and said, "You want this, don't you? The hate is *swelling* in you now."

He's right, Luke thought. *I hate him for everything he is, and everything he's done.*

"Take your Jedi weapon," the Emperor continued. "Use it. I am unarmed. Strike me down with it. Give in to your *anger*."

Luke turned away from the Emperor. *I won't give in. I won't.*

The Emperor continued, "With each passing moment you make yourself more my servant."

"No!" Luke shouted as he spun to glare at the evil wretch.

"It is unavoidable," the Emperor leered. "It is your destiny. You, like your father, are now *mine*!"

CHAPTER 11

Princess Leia, Han Solo, Chewbacca, and the Rebel commandos were led out of the bunker by their Imperial captors. Outside, they found the other members of their strike team standing together with their hands clasped behind their heads. They were surrounded by more than a hundred Imperial troops. One captured commando was especially conspicuous: He had obtained a scout trooper uniform before being apprehended, and he still wore the armor, minus the helmet. Obviously, he'd failed in his effort to infiltrate the Imperial soldiers.

An 8.6-meter-tall, two-legged All Terrain Scout Transport walker loomed above the soldiers; the AT-ST's pilot was visible atop the vehicle, his upper body rising through the hatch of the command cabin. Although not as tall as four-legged AT-AT walkers, the AT-ST was still an intimidating vehicle, especially since its blaster cannons were trained on the Rebels.

Leia spotted another AT-ST lurch past the trees on the ridge from which the Rebels had first glimpsed the bunker. *It was all a trap*, Leia realized. She thought of the Bothan spies who'd died in their effort to acquire and deliver the secret data regarding the new Death Star to the Alliance. *The Bothans were pawns. Everything — the data, the stolen Imperial shuttle, the clearance code for the shield passage — was a scheme to bring the Rebel fleet to Endor.*

"All right, move it!" said a stormtrooper behind Leia. "I said move it! Go on!" As Leia's group walked over to join the other Rebels, Leia glanced at Han. From his stunned expression, she knew he was thinking the same thing: Their situation was hopeless. They were more surprised than relieved when they heard a familiar voice call out from the forest, just beyond the clearing where they stood.

"Hello!" shouted C-3PO as he stepped out from behind a tall tree's wide trunk to stand beside R2-D2. "I say, over there! Were you looking for me?" The droids moved back behind the tree.

Chewbacca howled at the droids, urging them to run. Leia thought, *The droids are up to something. But what?*

The bunker commander turned to a squad of stormtroopers and said, "Bring those two down here."

"Let's go," said the stormtrooper squad leader. The white-armored troops headed off into the forest.

As the stormtroopers approached the droids, C-3PO turned to R2-D2 and said, "Well, they're on their way. Artoo, are you sure this was a good idea?"

The stormtroopers ran up and aimed their blaster rifles at the droids. "Freeze!" said the squad leader. "Don't move!"

"We surrender," C-3PO said, raising his hands.

But just as the stormtroopers were about to seize the droids, a band of Ewoks jumped down from the surrounding bushes. The Ewoks carried clubs, stones, knives, and spears, and every one of them had been itching to fight the invaders who'd cut down so many trees on their world. Their attack was swift and ferocious, and most of the stormtrooper squad fell without knowing what had hit them.

"Ohhh!" C-3PO cried as the brave Ewoks pummeled the stormtroopers. "Stand back, Artoo."

R2-D2 looked up to see Wicket arrive with Logray, Chief Chirpa, Teebo, and a small army of Ewoks. Wicket waved to the droids and chittered.

In a nearby tree, an Ewok raised a hollowed horn to his lips and sounded a battle call. The call was heard and repeated by an Ewok in another tree. Then the Imperials and Rebels were mutually astonished when hundreds of Ewoks rose from the bushes that surrounded the bunker's perimeter.

Most of the Ewoks wielded wooden bows. The

archers took quick but careful aim, then released a flurry of stone-tipped arrows at the Imperial soldiers.

Stormtroopers screamed and dived for cover. Han grabbed the nearest stormtrooper and flung him hard into another. Chewbacca did the same. Leia saw her blaster amidst a pile of confiscated weapons and snatched it up fast. She kicked a stormtrooper aside, then raised her blaster at the AT-ST pilot who hadn't been fast enough to lower himself into his vehicle. Leia fired, disabling the pilot.

The other Rebels quickly engaged the stormtroopers in hand-to-hand combat and took back their blaster rifles. As the clearing outside the bunker became rapidly littered with white-armored bodies and fallen weapons, several stormtrooper squads returned fire at the Ewoks. Most of the furry archers went scrambling into the woods, and the squads went after them. A pair of scout troopers hopped on their speeder bikes and joined in the pursuit.

Han spotted his blaster on the ground. He picked it up, knocked yet another stormtrooper aside, then moved fast alongside Leia, heading for the bunker's open doorway. But as they neared the bunker, the door slid shut to seal off the entrance. They dived against the recessed door as Imperial laserfire tore around their position. Most of the stormtroopers had gone after the Ewoks; Han and Leia fired back at the ones who hadn't.

In the woods, the stormtroopers fired at anything that moved. But despite their superior firepower, they rarely found their targets; the forest's density made it difficult to get a clear shot at anything, and the troopers frequently lost their balance on the uneven terrain.

The Ewoks exploited the stormtroopers' disadvantages at every opportunity. Swinging from vines and leaping out from behind bushes, they knocked the troopers off their feet and sent them tumbling down hills and into sinkholes, where they were met by more Ewoks with stones, clubs, and axes.

The AT-ST walkers proved to be a greater challenge for the Ewoks. Each armor-plated walker was equipped with maneuverable blaster cannons and a concussion-grenade launcher, and the pilots and gunners did their best to keep the Ewoks running. As a group of Ewoks scurried out of the way from a cannon-firing walker, they saw two of their fellows soaring high above the forest floor in stick-framed, leather-winged gliders. Both of the daring flyers carried stones.

As one flyer swooped over the walker, he dropped a stone that merely bounced off the vehicle's upper hull. The other flying Ewok had more success when he unloaded two stones onto the heads of stormtroopers. But as one trooper collapsed to the ground, his blaster fired a stray shot that went straight up and punched a hole through the second glider's wing. The Ewok shrieked as his glider spiralled out of control and crashed near the base of a large tree.

The fallen Ewok's allies raced to pull him out of the path of an oncoming walker, then slung a vine across the ground and held tight to the vine's ends in an effort to trip the vehicle. But when one of the walker's footpads snagged the vine, the Ewoks were instead yanked off their feet and dragged across the ground. Releasing the vine, they rushed to see if their nearby comrades had readied the catapults.

Elsewhere, Wicket had hastily enlisted with a division of Ewoks who hunted with bolas. They waited in the bushes until a group of stormtroopers rushed toward their position, then stood up, swung the bolas over their furry heads, and released the stone-weighted ropes at their targets. The bolas whipped around the troopers' heads, shattering their helmets and breaking bones. Wicket gave it his best try, but wound up getting tangled in his own bola and knocked himself down. Luckily, only his ego was bruised.

Back at the bunker, Leia reached for the control panel that was set within the doorway's frame. The door wouldn't open. "The code's changed," she said. "We need Artoo!"

Han looked below the control panel, found a socket, and said, "Here's the terminal."

The stormtroopers hadn't confiscated Leia's comlink, probably because they'd assumed it wouldn't be of any further use to her. They were wrong. She pulled the device from her pocket, switched it on, and said, "Artoo, where are you? We need you at the bunker right away."

R2-D2 was still with C-3PO, watching the Ewoks fight the stormtroopers, when he received Leia's transmitted communication. The astromech beeped to the golden droid, then moved away from beside the tree where they'd been standing.

"Going?" C-3PO said with alarm. "What do you mean, you're going? But — but going where, Artoo? No, wait! Artoo!" Artoo kept moving, and C-3PO hurried after him. "Oh, this is no time for heroics. Come back!"

In the woods, the Ewoks loaded heavy stones onto primitive catapults, then fired at an AT-ST walker. The stones flew past the trees and hammered at the walker's command compartment, but barely left a dent. Then the command compartment rotated to aim its cannons and fired back. The Ewoks fled as their catapult was blasted to bits.

The battle against the Empire didn't seem to be going much better in space. The Rebel fleet was greatly outnumbered. As more starfighters were lost to TIE interceptors, all Lando could do was fire at Imperial ships and try to stay alive.

Through the *Falcon*'s cockpit window, he sighted Wedge's X-wing. "Watch yourself, Wedge!" Lando shouted into his comlink. "Three from above!"

Wedge saw the three TIE fighters on his scopes and said, "Red Three, Red Two, pull in!"

The other pilots did as ordered and went after the TIE fighters. Red Two blasted one into spacedust and said, "Got it!"

Red Three said, "Three of them coming in, twenty degrees!"

"Cut to the left!" Wedge said. "I'll take the leader!" A moment later, Wedge fired his cannons and the lead TIE fighter was gone. Another TIE fighter zoomed in on Wedge's tail. Wedge sent his X-wing into a tight bank away from a Mon Cal cruiser. His pursuer failed to execute the bank and exploded against the larger ship's hull.

Wedge saw three more TIE fighters veer past his ship. He said, "They're heading for the medical frigate."

Lando steered the *Falcon* through a complete roll as he fired at one of the three TIE fighters. The TIE fighter exploded, and Lando went after the other two. As he wrapped around the medical frigate, the soldier who was serving as his navigator said from behind, "Pressure steady."

More laserfire spat out from the *Falcon*'s cannons, and two more TIE fighters exploded. But as Lando started to loop back to the medical frigate, he noticed the Star Destroyers had continued to maintain their distance from the battle. He said, "Only the fighters are attacking. I wonder what those Star Destroyers are waiting for."

On the main bridge of the Super Star Destroyer *Executor*, Admiral Piett and the Imperial Fleet Commander stood before the bridge's wide viewport and watched the battle that raged near the Death Star. Another officer approached them from the walkway that bisected the bridge and said, "We're in attack position now, sir."

"Hold here," Piett ordered.

"We're not going to attack?" asked the Fleet Commander, surprised.

"I have my orders from the Emperor himself," Piett stated with pride. "He has something special planned. We only need to keep them from escaping."

On the Death Star, the Emperor, Darth Vader, and a mortified Luke continued to watch the warring starships in the distance. From his throne, the Emperor said, "As you can see, my young apprentice, your friends have *failed*. Now witness the firepower of this fully armed and operational battle station." The Emperor pressed a button on his throne's armrest and said into his comlink, "Fire at will, Commander."

Luke, in shock, glanced at the Emperor, then returned his gaze to the Rebel fleet.

In the Death Star control room, buttons were pressed and switches were thrown. A black-helmeted Imperial gunner reached overhead and pulled a lever. Commander Jerjerrod gave the command: "Fire!"

The giant laserdish on the completed half of the Death Star began to glow. Then a powerful beam shot out toward the Rebel fleet and smashed into a Mon Cal cruiser. The cruiser exploded in a blinding flash.

The power of the explosion rocked the Rebel fleet. Inside the *Millennium Falcon*'s cockpit, Lando was stunned.

"That blast came from the Death Star!" he exclaimed. "That thing's operational! *Home One*, this is Gold Leader."

"We saw it," Admiral Ackbar answered. "All craft prepare to retreat."

Lando said, "You won't get another chance at this, Admiral."

"We have no choice, General Calrissian," Ackbar replied. "Our cruisers can't repel firepower of that magnitude."

"Han will have that shield down," Lando promised. "We've got to give him more time."

On Endor, Leia, Han, and a small group of Rebel commandos fought desperately to maintain their position outside the bunker that led to the shield generator control station. Four stormtroopers had found cover behind a fallen tree on the ridge that overlooked the bunker, maintaining a definite tactical advantage as they fired down at the Rebels below. Han was wishing he had a grenade to lob at the troopers when he saw a band of spear-wielding Ewoks leap out from the bushes above and behind the ridge. Pouncing quickly, the Ewoks made quick work of the white-armored soldiers.

But the bunker door remained closed. Leia wondered, *Where's Artoo?*

Just then, C-3PO called out, "We're coming!"

Han and Leia saw the droids moving on the ridge, trying to make their way down to the bunker, as an enemy-fired laserbolt streaked past R2-D2's domed head. Han traced the angle of fire to spot the shooter: a stormtrooper hiding behind some nearby bushes. Han raised his blaster, fired, and struck the shooter squarely in the middle of his helmet. The trooper fell back against the ground.

"Come on! Come on!" Han shouted to the droids.

More stormtroopers fired at the bunker. C-3PO ran up beside Leia as R2-D2 scooted over next to Han. Positioning himself beside the doorway's computer terminal, R2-D2 extended his computer interface arm and plugged into the terminal socket.

C-3PO said, "Oh, Artoo, hurry!"

But before the astromech could open the door, a stormtrooper fired a laserbolt that struck directly in front of him. The droid screeched as the blast launched him backward from the terminal to the far side of the doorway, where he slammed against the door's metal frame. Han sighted R2-D2's attacker and fired his blaster; the stormtrooper fell to the ground.

C-3PO stepped beside R2-D2, then backed away as an electrical surge suddenly coursed through and over the astromech's body. Artoo screeched again, then every compartment on his body popped open to deploy his many tool-tipped appendages.

"My goodness!" C-3PO cried as smoke poured out from his friend's domed head. "Artoo, why did you have to be so brave?"

Han and Leia gaped at R2-D2's disabled form, then Han said, "Well, I suppose I could hot-wire this thing." He turned for the door's control panel.

"I'll cover you," Leia said. She began firing at the stormtroopers, allowing Han to concentrate on the door's mechanisms. Sparks flew as he broke the control panel open and fumbled with some exposed wires.

Leia had no idea what was happening with the Rebel fleet, but she knew that if she and Han failed to knock out the energy shield generator, the battle would be lost.

The Death Star fired its superlaser again, and another Mon Cal cruiser was instantly vaporized. As Wedge Antilles raced his X-wing away from the explosion, he wasn't sure if he'd heard Lando Calrissian's last message correctly, and asked him to repeat.

From the *Millennium Falcon*, Lando shouted, "Yes! I said closer! Move as close as you can and engage those Star Destroyers at point-blank range."

On the *Home One*, Admiral Ackbar heard Lando's transmission and said, "At that close range we won't last long against those Star Destroyers."

Lando replied, "We'll last longer than we will against that Death Star — and we might just take a few of them with us."

Ackbar agreed with Lando's improvised plan; *Home One* and the remaining cruisers began speeding toward the Star Destroyers. The Rebels were practically on top of the enemy ships when they opened fire on the Star Destroyers' control bridges and communication towers.

TIE fighters zoomed in to defend the Imperial warships and went after the Rebel starfighters with even greater maliciousness. An X-wing pilot blasted at a Destroyer's port-side deflector-shield generator dome and shouted, "She's gonna blow!" The dome exploded, but a moment later, TIE fighters fired at the X-wing and it blossomed into a ball of fire.

"I'm hit!" cried a Rebel pilot from his flaming Y-wing. The Y-wing spiraled away from the TIE fighters and smashed into a Star Destroyer.

On the Death Star, the Emperor was unconcerned by the way the battle had shifted to the Star Destroyers. He gazed at Luke, who remained by the circular window, and said, "Your fleet is lost. And your friends on the Endor moon will not survive. There is no escape, my young apprentice."

Luke glanced at Darth Vader. He thought, *If there's even a trace of Anakin Skywalker left, he wouldn't stand by and allow this to continue.*

But all Darth Vader did was return Luke's gaze.

The Emperor opened his yellow eyes and said, "The Alliance will die . . . as will your friends."

Luke glared at the Emperor and wished the wretched man would choke on his words.

"Good," the Emperor said, closing his yellow eyes and smiling. "I can *feel* your anger. I am defenseless."

Luke glanced at his lightsaber, still resting near the Emperor's right hand on the throne's armrest.

"Take your weapon!" the Emperor challenged. "Strike me down with all of your *hatred* and your journey toward the dark side will be complete."

Luke turned away, trying to resist the temptation to kill the Emperor. Then he thought, *But if I don't kill him, how many more innocent people will die?*

Luke moved fast, turning to face the Emperor as he used the Force to make his lightsaber fly from the throne's armrest to his waiting hand. His lightsaber blazed to life and he swung fast at the Emperor's head.

Luke's lightsaber never reached its target. Darth Vader's red-bladed lightsaber ignited a split second after Luke's, and Vader deftly blocked the attack.

Seeing the two lightsabers crossed mere centimeters in front of his horrible face, Emperor Palpatine cackled. He hadn't seen a lightsaber duel in years, and was now delighted by the prospect of watching a father and son try to kill each other.

I won't kill you, father, Luke thought. *I won't!*

Then Vader pushed Luke back away from the Emperor, and Luke was suddenly fighting for his life.

On Endor, AT-ST walkers continued to prowl the forest and fire at the scurrying Ewoks. As a walker moved past a tree-covered hillside, two Ewoks looked up at the tallest and furriest new member of their tribe: Chewbacca. The Wookiee reached for a long vine that dangled from the treetops, then barked to his short allies.

The two Ewoks threw their arms and legs around him and clung tight as he seized the vine. Chewbacca howled a battle cry as he leaped away from the hill, carrying the Ewoks with him. They swung over the forest floor and landed with a loud thud on top of the nearest Imperial walker.

Inside the walker's cockpit, the pilot and gunner heard the noise above their helmeted heads. A moment later, the gunner sighted an upside-down Ewok hanging in front of the pilot's viewport. The gunner pointed and said, "Look!"

The walker's pilot looked to the viewport. The Ewok chuckled, then slid out of view. The pilot said to the gunner, "Get him off of there!"

The gunner stood and pushed up the roof-mounted entry hatch. When the hatch was fully opened, Chewbacca reached down and hauled the gunner straight out of the cockpit. The gunner screamed as he was hurled from the top of the vehicle.

Before the walker's pilot realized what had happened, the two Ewoks leaped down into the cockpit and clubbed him. Shoving the pilot's body into the cramped compartment behind the seats, the Ewoks reached for the steering controls.

Chewbacca was nearly thrown from the walker's roof as the vehicle lurched forward, but he bent down and quickly eased himself through the hatch. The Ewoks made room for him as he settled into the pilot's seat.

Through the viewports, Chewbacca saw another walker nearby; it was firing at a group of fleeing Ewoks. Chewbacca and his companions decided to put a stop to it.

The Wookiee guided his walker through the woods, then fired the blaster cannons at the other walker. The enemy walker's command cabin exploded, spraying metal in all directions. When the Ewoks on the ground looked back at the vehicle, all that remained was its two legs and a shattered drive engine. The Ewoks cheered.

Without breaking his walker's stride, Chewbacca aimed his cannons at the Imperial ground troops and fired. Laserbolts tore through the forest, and the stormtroopers ran to escape the barrage.

The explosions drew the attention of the remaining two scout troopers. As they flew in tandem formation past the trees on their speeder bikes, an Ewok tossed a looped vine into the path of the scout at the rear. The other end of the long, heavy vine had been anchored to the base of a tree; when the thrown loop lassoed the bike's steering vanes, the snagged bike began whipping around the tree at high speed. The bike carried its rider on a rapid clockwise trip until the vine was completely wrapped around the tree's trunk and the bike crashed and exploded.

The last scout trooper was also done in by a well-placed vine, which the Ewoks had stretched a short distance above the ground between two trees. Striking the vine, the scout was knocked from his saddle while his bike hurtled forward and collided with another tree.

The Ewoks continued to fight with cunning innovation, using the forest's natural resources against the Imperial invaders. When they saw two Imperial walkers moving swiftly through the woods, they simultaneously released two vine-suspended logs from the treetops; the massive logs swung like twin hammers, smashing into both sides of the first walker's command cabin. As the second walker moved past the bottom of a hill, Ewoks stationed at the top of the hill unleashed stacked timber; the walker was unable to maintain its balance against the avalanche of rolling logs. Both walkers exploded.

With most of their walkers destroyed, the Imperial ground troops were fast becoming overwhelmed by their adversaries. No matter where they ran, the Ewoks were waiting for them with stones and arrows.

Back at the bunker, R2-D2 was still out of commission and C-3PO cringed in the doorway. Leia continued to fire at stormtroopers, keeping them at bay while Han worked on hot-wiring the door.

Han said, "I think I got it. I got it!" The wires sparked and a connection was made, but instead of opening the access to the bunker, a second blast door slid into place in front of the first.

As Han frowned and turned back to the wires again, Leia exchanged shots with stormtroopers in the bushes. Suddenly, a laserbolt struck her left shoulder. Leia cried out in pain and fell against the doorway.

Han didn't even try to find Leia's shooter. Trying to protect her, he grabbed her and eased her down so she was sitting with her back against the base of the door's control panel. C-3PO stepped near them and said, "Oh, Princess Leia, are you all right?"

Han crouched to face Leia and checked her wounded arm. He said, "Let's see."

"It's not bad," Leia said, slightly breathless.

"Freeze!" said one of two stormtroopers, who'd appeared suddenly behind Han. Both troopers had their blaster rifles aimed at Han's back. Han didn't move, and kept his eyes on Leia.

"Oh, dear," C-3PO said.

"Don't move!" commanded the stormtrooper.

Han didn't budge. Leia shifted only slightly, just enough so Han could see that her right hand still grasped her blaster pistol. Han realized his own body blocked the stormtroopers' view of Leia's blaster. Then he returned his gaze to Leia. Speaking just loud enough so only she could hear, he said, "I love you."

"I know," she replied.

"Hands up!" said one of the stormtroopers. "Stand up!"

Han raised his hands and stood up slowly, then turned. Leia's blaster spat twice, and each shot pierced the stormtroopers' armor-plated chests. They collapsed beside the bunker.

As Han turned toward Leia, he saw an AT-ST

walker approaching. The walker came to a stop with its cannons aimed at Han. Han raised his hands and said to Leia, "Stay back."

Han bravely faced the walker, and was astonished when the hatch opened at the vehicle's roof and Chewbacca stuck his head out. The Wookiee barked triumphantly to Han.

"Chewie!" Han said, lowering his hands and grinning from ear to ear. Then he gestured toward Leia and said, "Get down here! She's wounded!" But before Chewbacca could move, Han said, "No, wait . . ." Then he turned to Leia and said, "I got an idea."

CHAPTER 13

On the Death Star, Luke and Darth Vader were engaged in a duel that was even more vicious than their battle on Cloud City. Luke had grown stronger since their last encounter, and his skill with his lightsaber had improved greatly. As they swung at each other in the Emperor's throne room, Luke sensed the advantage had shifted to him.

Luke drove Vader back to the stairway that descended to the turbolifts, then kicked out with his left leg, knocking Vader from the upper platform. Vader groaned as he flipped over backward and landed on the metal floor below.

From his throne, the Emperor watched the fight with glee. "Good," he said. "Use your aggressive feelings, boy! Let the hate flow through you."

Standing at the top of the stairway, Luke watched Vader rise on the lower platform. Vader said, "Obi-Wan has taught you well."

Luke deactivated his lightsaber.

"I will not fight you, father," he said.

Vader kept his lightsaber activated as he slowly ascended the stairs. His movement was slightly stiff and robotic, as if he were moving on damaged legs without feeling any pain. Luke wondered if Ben was right about Vader, that he was more machine than man. Then he thought, *No! Darth Vader may be a mechanical monster, but not my father. Not Anakin!*

When Vader was almost beside Luke, he said, "You are unwise to lower your defenses." He brought his lightsaber up fast, but Luke ignited his own lightsaber in time and blocked the attack. Vader swung again and again, and Luke parried each blow. Then their blades met and they maintained the contact, keeping their lightsabers braced against each other. Over the humming of the lightsabers, Luke heard Vader's labored breathing and realized, *He's getting tired.*

Vader broke the contact and swung hard at Luke, but Luke evaded the red blur of his opponent's weapon and jumped backward, landing in a duty post that was encircled by eight illuminated control consoles. As Vader brought his lightsaber up between two console pedestals, Luke deactivated his own lightsaber and leaped high toward the ceiling, executing a reverse flip that delivered him to a catwalk that stretched above the throne room. Landing on his feet, Luke looked down from the catwalk to see Vader, still standing beside the duty post, breathing hard.

Luke said, "Your thoughts betray you, father. I feel the good in you . . . the conflict."

"There is no conflict," Vader said.

Luke moved across the catwalk so he was positioned above the stairway. Gazing down at Vader, he said, "You couldn't bring yourself to kill me before, and I don't believe you'll destroy me now."

"You underestimate the power of the dark side," Vader answered from below. "If you will not fight, then you will meet your destiny." His right arm moved fast, and he hurled his still-activated lightsaber up at Luke.

Luke ducked the lightsaber, but its blade cut through the supports that held the catwalk. Luke felt the catwalk drop, and sparks showered around him as the metal supports tore from the ceiling and he tumbled to the floor below. Uninjured, he rolled under the Emperor's elevated platform and ducked into a dark alcove.

Vader's lightsaber had deactivated after it had sliced through the catwalk supports. As the Dark Lord of the Sith descended the stairs, he extended his hand and his lightsaber traveled through the air to return to his grip. Behind him, the Emperor rose from his seat, laughed, and said, "Good. Good."

Vader activated his lightsaber and went hunting for his son.

Outside, Lando Calrissian's plan was working: the Death Star had not fired at the Rebel fleet since the Rebels had brought the battle into the midst of the Star Destroyers. However, the Star Destroyers were openly firing at the Rebel cruisers and starfighters, and Lando knew the Alliance's fate now depended on whether his allies on Endor could knock out the Death Star's energy shield.

From the *Millennium Falcon*'s cockpit, Lando sighted TIE fighters angling toward a Rebel cruiser. He said into his comlink, "Watch out. Squad at point oh-six."

Gray Leader said, "I'm on it, Gold Leader."

Red Two swooped in to lend a hand, and the TIE fighters were decimated. From his X-wing, Wedge Antilles exclaimed, "Good shot, Red Two."

"Now . . . come on, Han, old buddy," Lando said to himself. "Don't let me down."

On Endor, in the same control room within the bunker where the Rebel strike team had been apprehended, the control room commander, his second commander, a security officer, and three seated controllers believed they were winning the battle. When a transmission from an AT-ST walker was received, all six men turned to see the image of the walker's pilot on the room's main viewscreen.

"It's over, Commander," the helmeted pilot announced. Holding his comlink over his mouth, he continued, "The Rebels have been routed. They're fleeing into the woods. We need reinforcements to continue the pursuit."

The officers and controllers looked away from the viewscreen to the control room commander. He could see from their excited expressions that his men were eager to go after the Rebels. They could see that he was looking forward to it, too. "Send three squads to help," said the commander. "Open the back door."

"Sir," said the second commander, and carried out the order.

They had no idea that the helmeted pilot on their viewscreen had been Han Solo.

The bunker door opened and the Imperial troops rushed out. They were surprised to find themselves suddenly surrounded by armed Rebels and Ewoks. Most of the Ewoks carried spears and bows and arrows, but some brandished blaster rifles they'd confiscated from fallen stormtroopers.

The Imperial soldiers turned to face the open door behind them. Han and Chewbacca stood at either side. Han grinned at the duped troops, then he and Chewbacca entered the bunker with several Rebel commandos. The commandos carried the explosive charges they'd retrieved from the stormtroopers.

Arriving in the control room, the Rebels quickly planted high-powered proton grenades onto the control panels and beside the turbine generator. Chewbacca growled, urging everyone to hurry.

Han turned to a Rebel commando and said, "Throw me another charge." Han caught the grenade, twisted its arming mechanism, and used the device's magnetic plate to secure it to the ceiling. When the last charge was in place, the Rebels left the control room and ran as fast as they could for the bunker's exit.

Darth Vader stalked the low-ceilinged area below the elevated platform in the Emperor's throne room. Holding his lightsaber ready, he searched for his son in the semi-darkness and said, "You cannot hide forever, Luke."

From the shadows, Luke answered, "I will not fight you."

"Give yourself to the dark side," Vader urged. "It is the only way you can save your friends."

Luke closed his eyes. *I'm sorry, Leia and Han. I'd do anything to save you, but I must resist the dark side.* Suddenly, Luke felt a dull ache in his head, and sensed that Vader was using the Force to probe his mind.

"Yes, your thoughts betray you," Vader spoke, confirming Luke's suspicion. "Your feelings for them are strong. Especially for . . ."

Luke tried to block his thoughts — and failed.

"*Sister!*" Vader said. "So . . . you have a twin sister. Your feelings have now betrayed her, too. Obi-Wan was wise to hide her from me. Now his failure is complete. If you will not turn to the dark side, then perhaps she will."

"*No!*" Luke screamed in anger as he ignited his lightsaber and rushed at Vader. Sparks flew as they traded blows in the cramped area, and Luke felt the hatred within him build with each passing second. *You'll never take Leia, and you'll never take me!*

He kept swinging, forcing Vader to retreat from under the platform until they arrived at the short bridge that overlooked the elevator shaft. Vader fell back against the bridge's railing, then was knocked to his knees. As he raised his lightsaber to block another onslaught, Luke slashed through Vader's right hand, severing it at the wrist. Metal and electronic parts flew from Vader's shattered stump, and his lightsaber clattered uselessly away, rolling over the edge of the bridge and into the apparently bottomless shaft below.

Luke angled his lightsaber at Vader's throat, then held the blade there, watching Vader's struggling form.

On the stairway behind Luke, the Emperor was unable to contain himself. "Good! Your hate has made you powerful. Now, fulfill your destiny and take your father's place at *my* side!"

Luke knew what the Emperor expected. *He wants me to kill Vader. He wants me to kill my own father.* Luke looked at his father's mechanical hand, then to his own black-gloved right hand. *Am I becoming like my father? Is that my destiny after all?*

Then Luke made the decision for which he had spent a lifetime preparing. He deactivated his lightsaber, turned to the Emperor, and said "Never!" Luke flung his lightsaber aside and stood there unarmed.

The Emperor scowled.

"I'll never turn to the dark side," Luke vowed. "You've failed, Your Highness. I am a Jedi, like my father before me."

With immeasurable displeasure, the Emperor said, "So be it . . . *Jedi.*"

CHAPTER 14

Han Solo ran out of the Imperial bunker shouting, "Move! Move! Move!" Chewbacca and the other Rebels ran away and dived for cover. A moment later, the bunker exploded, followed by the turbine generator and the reactor core. The generator tower was suddenly consumed by a series of explosions, and the enormous dish-shaped shield projector array came crashing down to the ground.

The destruction of the moon-based Imperial outpost was immediately acknowledged by the space cruiser *New Home*'s Mon Calamari crew. Admiral Ackbar announced, "The shield is down! Commence attack on the Death Star's main reactor."

From the *Millennium Falcon*, Lando Calrissian responded, "We're on our way. Red Group, Gold Group, all fighters follow me." Lando looked to Nien Nunb and laughed. "Told you they'd do it!" Nunb laughed, too.

Wedge Antilles' X-wing, two A-wings, another X-wing, and a single Y-wing starfighter swung away from the Rebel fleet. The starfighters followed the *Falcon*, which flew straight and fast for the unfinished superstructure of the Death Star.

In the Emperor's throne room, Darth Vader remained lying against the railing on the bridge above the elevator shaft. Vader had known Emperor Palpatine long enough to know what would happen next. He watched the Emperor descend to the bottom of the stairs and face Luke.

The Emperor said, "If you will not be turned, you will be *destroyed*." Then he raised his arms and extended his gnarled fingers toward Luke. Blinding bolts of blue lightning shot from the Emperor's hands, and Luke was suddenly enveloped by crackling bands of energy. He tried to deflect the lightning but was so overwhelmed that his knees buckled. He collapsed onto some canisters near the bridge's railing.

As the Emperor continued to strike Luke with energized bolts, Vader struggled to his feet. Badly wounded, he moved slowly to stand beside his Master.

Sneering at Luke, the Emperor said, "Young *fool* . . . only now, at the end, do you understand."

More blue lightning coursed over and through Luke. He fought to remain conscious and clutched at a canister to keep from falling into the adjacent shaft.

"Your feeble skills are no match for the power of the dark side," the Emperor leered. "You have paid the price of your lack of vision." He released another bombardment of power at Luke, who writhed on the floor in unbearable pain.

Using the last of his strength, Luke lifted his arm, and reached out toward Vader. "Father, please," Luke groaned. "Help me."

Vader could see that Luke was on the verge of death. He looked to the Emperor, then back to Luke, who had curled into a fetal position on the floor.

"Now, young Skywalker . . ." the Emperor snarled, "you will die."

Luke had not imagined pain beyond what he had already suffered, but then he was hit by a wave of power that was even more staggering. His harsh screams echoed across the throne room.

Beside the Emperor, Darth Vader continued to stand and watch. He looked to the Emperor again, then back to Luke.

And then, in a moment, something changed. Perhaps he remembered something heard in his youth a long time ago: an ancient prophecy of the Chosen One who would bring balance to the Force. Perhaps the vague outlines of someone named Shmi and a Jedi named Qui-Gon struggled to the surface of his consciousness. The most powerful, the most repressed thought of all could have emerged from the darkness:

Padmé . . . and her undying love for someone he once knew well. And despite all the terrible, unspeakable things he'd done in his life, he suddenly realized he could not stand by and allow the Emperor to kill their son. And in that moment, he was no longer Darth Vader.

He was Anakin Skywalker.

He grabbed the Emperor from behind. The impossibly wretched Sith Lord gaped and squirmed in his embrace, continuing to release blue lightning, but the bolts veered away from Luke and arced back to strike the Sith Lords.

Dazed, Luke looked up to see the lightning travel through Vader and the Emperor. A burst of high-energy photons made Vader's own damaged skull briefly visible through his armored helmet. Somehow, despite his severed hand, Vader had managed to lift the Emperor high over his head. With one final burst of his once-venerated strength, Darth Vader hurled the Emperor into the elevator shaft, then collapsed at the shaft's edge.

Emperor Palpatine screamed as his body plunged down the seemingly bottomless shaft. When he was almost beyond sight, his body exploded, releasing dark energy and creating a rush of air up through the throne room.

From where he lay, Luke could tell by the rasping rattle from Vader's helmet that his breathing apparatus was broken. Luke crawled the short distance to his father's side and pulled him away from the edge of the abyss.

The *Millennium Falcon* and the Rebel starfighters flew low over the Death Star's surface. From his X-wing's cockpit, Wedge sighted the wide exhaust port that would be their entry point through the space station's superstructure to reach the reactor core. Wedge said, "I'm going in."

Wedge's X-wing dived into the exhaust port, followed by one of the two A-wings.

Lando said, "Here goes nothing," and guided the *Falcon* into the exhaust port with the other Rebel fighters right behind him. But then three standard TIE fighters zoomed in after the Rebels — and they were quickly followed by a trio of dagger-winged TIE interceptors.

At its present stage of construction, the Death Star's superstructure resembled a series of interconnected mazelike tunnels. Wedge maintained his lead position, flying past crisscrossing girders and lift tubes at an alarming speed. Despite the fact that the *Falcon* was bulkier than the single-pilot fighters, Lando was experienced with handling the old freighter through tight areas, and followed Wedge and the A-wing pilot without difficulty.

When Wedge wrapped around a tight corner to

enter a different tunnel, all the Rebel ships made the turn. The six TIE fighters followed, but one Imperial pilot lost control and collided with a large metal pipe that ran the length of the tunnel; his fighter exploded, but the others increased speed to pursue the Rebel ships.

Lando adjusted a switch on his console, then said into his comlink, "Now lock on to the strongest power source. It should be the power generator."

"Form up," Wedge told the other fighters. "And stay alert. We could run out of space real fast."

Indeed, the tunnel appeared to be narrowing. As they continued to race for the reactor core, laserfire tore past them from behind. The X-wing at the rear of the group was hit and exploded in the tunnel.

Lando looked past the X-wing and A-wing in front of him and saw that the tunnel forked in two directions. Hoping to shake their Imperial pursuers, he said, "Split up and head back to the surface. And see if you can get a few of those TIE fighters to follow you."

"Copy, Gold Leader," answered an A-wing pilot.

At the tunnel juncture, Wedge went left and Lando followed him. The other Rebel starfighters veered to the right. Lando checked his scopes and saw there were now only two TIE interceptors behind him.

Wedge saw their route was becoming even more difficult to navigate, and he threw his X-wing into a short dive to avoid striking a low girder. Behind him, Lando attempted the same maneuver, but the *Falcon*'s oversized sensor dish smashed against the girder and broke free from the hull. Wincing at the sound of shredding metal, Lando said, "That was too close."

Nien Nunb agreed.

Beyond the Death Star, the battle between the Rebel and Imperial fleets raged on. When one Rebel commander suggested they retreat, Admiral Ackbar answered, "We've got to give those fighters more time. Concentrate all fire on that Super Star Destroyer."

Following Ackbar's order, the Rebel cruisers and remaining starfighters targeted the *Executor* and began firing. The Super Star Destroyer rapidly became battered by explosions. On the *Executor*'s bridge, Admiral Piett was standing beside an Imperial commander in front of the viewport, and they saw the damage being inflicted on their ship.

Piett was about to issue a command when a controller from the lower-level crew pit said, "Sir, we've lost our bridge deflector shield."

"Intensify the forward batteries," Piett ordered. "I don't want anything to get through." Returning his gaze to the viewport, Piett saw another explosion. Losing his composure, he shouted, "Intensify forward firepower!"

"Too late!" yelled the commander beside him, who saw an out-of-control A-wing spinning straight for the bridge.

The A-wing smashed into the *Executor*'s bridge and exploded, causing the entire ship to veer off course. Damage-control crews were unable to seize command using the auxiliary control centers, and the *Executor* was dragged into the Death Star's gravitational field. The other Star Destroyer crews watched in horror as the *Executor* plunged like an enormous knife into the Death Star and exploded.

For the first time since the battle had begun, the Death Star was rocked by explosions. Inside, Imperial troops ran in all directions, confused and desperate to escape. As one group ran past a hangar, they noticed a strange figure: a blonde young man dressed in black, who struggled to haul Darth Vader's body to the same *Lambda* shuttle that had transported them from Endor's forest moon. Not surprisingly, none of the Imperial soldiers offered to help Luke Skywalker.

Luke stumbled, too weak to support his father's heavy body any further. *Don't worry, father. I won't leave you here!* Trying not to cause more damage to his father's right arm, he dragged him across the hangar deck to the shuttle's landing ramp. He was only at the base of the ramp when he collapsed from the effort.

Vader lay prone against the ramp. From the corridor outside the hangar came the sound of more explosions. Breathing hard, Luke looked up to his father's masked visage.

"Luke," Vader gasped, "help me take this mask off."

Luke didn't have to look at the life systems computer on Vader's chestplate to know what his father was suggesting. Luke said, "But you'll die."

"Nothing can stop that now. Just for once . . . let me look on you . . . with my own eyes."

Slowly, hesitantly, Luke lifted the helmet, leaving the faceplate still secured over his father's face. Setting the helmet aside, he reached to the faceplate and carefully removed it from the black durasteel shell that wrapped around his neck. And then he saw his father's face for the first time.

His flesh was ghastly, deathly pale and brutally scarred. There were dark circles under his eyes, and from what Luke could see, it appeared his skull had been hideously damaged. Luke tried to conceal his initial shock, then found himself staring into his father's eyes. They were blue, like his own.

Anakin smiled weakly and said, "Now . . . go, my son. Leave me."

"No," Luke said, placing his hand on his father's shoulder. "You're coming with me. I'll not leave you here. I've got to save you."

Anakin smiled again. "You already have, Luke. You were right." Choking, he gasped, "You were right about me. Tell your sister . . . you were right."

Anakin slumped back against the ramp. Luke leaned over him and said, "Father . . . I won't leave you." Then Luke noticed that his father's breathing apparatus was no longer making any noise.

Anakin Skywalker was dead.

Wedge's X-wing and the *Millennium Falcon* flew out of the tunnel and entered the Death Star's reactor core. The Rebel pilots were immediately followed by the two TIE interceptors that had pursued them since they'd split off from the other starfighters.

The reactor core was an enormous circular chamber. At its center was the main reactor, a massive power transference assembly with a ceiling-mounted generator.

"There it is!" Wedge said.

"All right, Wedge," said Lando. "Go for the power regulator on the north tower."

"Copy, Gold Leader," Wedge replied. "I'm already on my way out."

Wedge angled toward the ceiling and fired proton torpedoes at the upper area of the power regulator, causing a series of small explosions. As Wedge looped around and away from the main reactor, Lando fired the *Falcon*'s missiles.

The missiles scored direct hits on the main reactor. Lando winced at the brilliant light of the blast, but never lost control as he followed Wedge's escape route. Behind him, one of the two TIE interceptors was struck by the explosive release of energy and was vaporized. As the remaining TIE interceptor accelerated in pursuit of the *Falcon*, the reactor's upper assembly began to crash down from the ceiling. Just as the *Falcon* sped back into the tunnel, the entire reactor core was filled with superheated gases that rushed after the starships and into the tunnel.

Lando followed Wedge's lead through the tunnel, retracing their path through the Death Star's superstructure at an even greater speed as they tried to outrun the explosion. Behind him, the TIE interceptor also increased speed.

Admiral Ackbar and his Mon Calamari officers saw the explosions that were tearing across the Imperial space station. Ackbar said, "Move the fleet away from the Death Star."

Fire and smoke filled the Death Star hangar, and a crashing gantry nearly smashed the front of the shuttle as it lifted from the deck. Seated behind its controls, Luke deftly turned the ship so it faced out, then hit the thrusters. He'd barely cleared the hangar doorway when the entire docking bay exploded behind him. Luke breathed a sigh of relief when he realized he'd made it.

A moment later, Wedge's X-wing hurtled out of the exhaust port and headed straight for the forest moon. He saw that the Rebel fleet had already moved to a safe position, distancing itself from the impending blast.

Behind the *Falcon*, the wave of intense heat caught up with the TIE interceptor and the ship was transformed into a fireball. This encouraged Lando to fly even faster. Through the cockpit window, he saw the star-filled hole at the end of the tunnel just as the space around the *Falcon* caught fire. A mass of jet flame geysered from the exhaust port, then the *Falcon* blasted through it and away from the Death Star. Lando let out a loud victory cry as he punched the thrusters.

The Death Star exploded. The blast was so brilliant and enormous that it could be seen from the forest moon's daylit hemisphere. There, the Ewoks and the Rebel ground troops cheered at the sight.

"They did it!" C-3PO cried with excitement. He was standing on a grassy hill with R2-D2, Chewbacca, and a group of Ewoks, and none of them could have been happier.

Nearby, Han was bandaging Leia's wounded arm. They looked up at the explosion's smoky remnants across the clear blue sky. His expression betraying his concern, Han turned to Leia and said, "I'm sure Luke wasn't on that thing when it blew."

Leia looked away from the explosion and smiled. "He wasn't. I can feel it."

Hesitantly, Han said, "You love him, don't you?"

Leia was puzzled by Han's question, but answered, "Yes."

"All right," Han said, putting on a brave face. "I understand. Fine. When he comes back, I won't get in the way."

Leia realized Han's misunderstanding and said, "Oh. No, it's not like that at all." She leaned closer to Han and said, "He's my *brother*."

Han was stunned by this news. Leia smiled, and they embraced.

EPILOGUE

Darkness had fallen on the forest moon when Luke carried a flaming torch to the logs he'd stacked in a clearing. He set the torch to the logs and they began to burn. On top of the pyre lay his father's armor; the image of Vader would burn away.

Standing alone, Luke watched the fire and felt the heat of its blaze. Although he had accomplished much that day, he couldn't help but feel a tremendous sense of loss. Not for Darth Vader, but for Anakin Skywalker, the father he'd barely known.

The flames rose high into the night. Fireworks exploded overhead, and then starfighters streaked across the sky. Luke realized his allies were celebrating.

And not just on Endor's moon, for news of the Rebel victory had spread quickly across the galaxy. Later, Luke would learn there had been fireworks over Cloud City, parades on Tatooine, and joyous public rallies on Naboo and Coruscant.

When the pyre had burned out, Luke went to find his friends.

High above the forest floor, a huge bonfire was the centerpiece of a wild celebration in the Ewok village square. All of the Rebels — even the droids — wound up dancing with the Ewoks, some of whom were enjoying the unusual percussive qualities of confiscated Imperial-issue helmets. Others hammered at the helmets just for fun.

Leia changed back into the clothes the Ewoks had made for her. Lando arrived and was enthusiastically greeted by Han and Chewbacca. Then Luke arrived and his friends rushed to greet and embrace him. Wedge and Nien Nunb were also warmly greeted by all.

Despite the happy reunion, Luke still felt distracted, his thoughts elsewhere. Stepping away from the others, he gazed out into the night and wondered, *Could I have done anything differently, or sooner, to have helped my father? I guess I'll never know.*

And then he saw them: two shimmering apparitions that appeared before him in the darkness. Yoda and Ben Kenobi. Then a third apparition materialized beside them — a figure whom he instinctively knew was a younger Anakin Skywalker, from the days before his Jedi father's fall, his features unscarred and . . . happy. Luke was right: He was a Jedi like his father before him. The apparitions smiled at Luke, silently telling him that the Force would be with him always.

Leia came to Luke's side and took his hand, then led him back to the others.

The celebration went on long into the night.